Disney DESCENDANTS

◄·°TWISTED FIELD TRIP°·►

DISNEY DESCENDANTS

◄·TWISTED FIELD TRIP·►

STORY BY
JEN VAUGHN, CARIN DAVIS, AND DELILAH S. DAWSON

SCRIPT BY
DELILAH S. DAWSON AND CARIN DAVIS

PENCILS BY
EGLE BARTOLINI AND ANNA CATTISH

INKS AND COLORS BY
ANNA CATTISH

LETTERS BY
CHRISTA MIESNER

EDITS BY
ELIZABETH BREI

GROUP EDITS BY
DENTON TIPTON

Special thanks to Jodi Hammerwold, Behnoosh Khalili, Manny Mederos, Miriam Ogawa,
Eugene Paraszczuk and Carlotta Quattrocolo.

For international rights, contact licensing@idwpublishing.c

Chris Ryall, President & Publisher/CCO • John Barber, Editor-in-Chief • Robbie Robbins, EVP/Sr. Art Director • Cara Morrison, Chief Financial Officer • Matthew Ruzic
Chief Accounting Officer • Anita Frazier, SVP of Sales and Marketing • David Hedgecock, Associate Publisher • Jerry Bennington, VP of New Product Developme
Lorelei Bunjes, VP of Digital Services • Justin Eisinger, Editorial Director, Graphic novels and Collections • Eric Moss, Sr. Director, Licensing & Business Developme
Ted Adams, IDW Founder

www.IDWPUBLISHING.com

Facebook: facebook.com/idwpublishing • Twitter: @idwpublishing • YouTube: youtube.com/idwpublishing
Tumblr: tumblr.idwpublishing.com • Instagram: instagram.com/idwpublishing

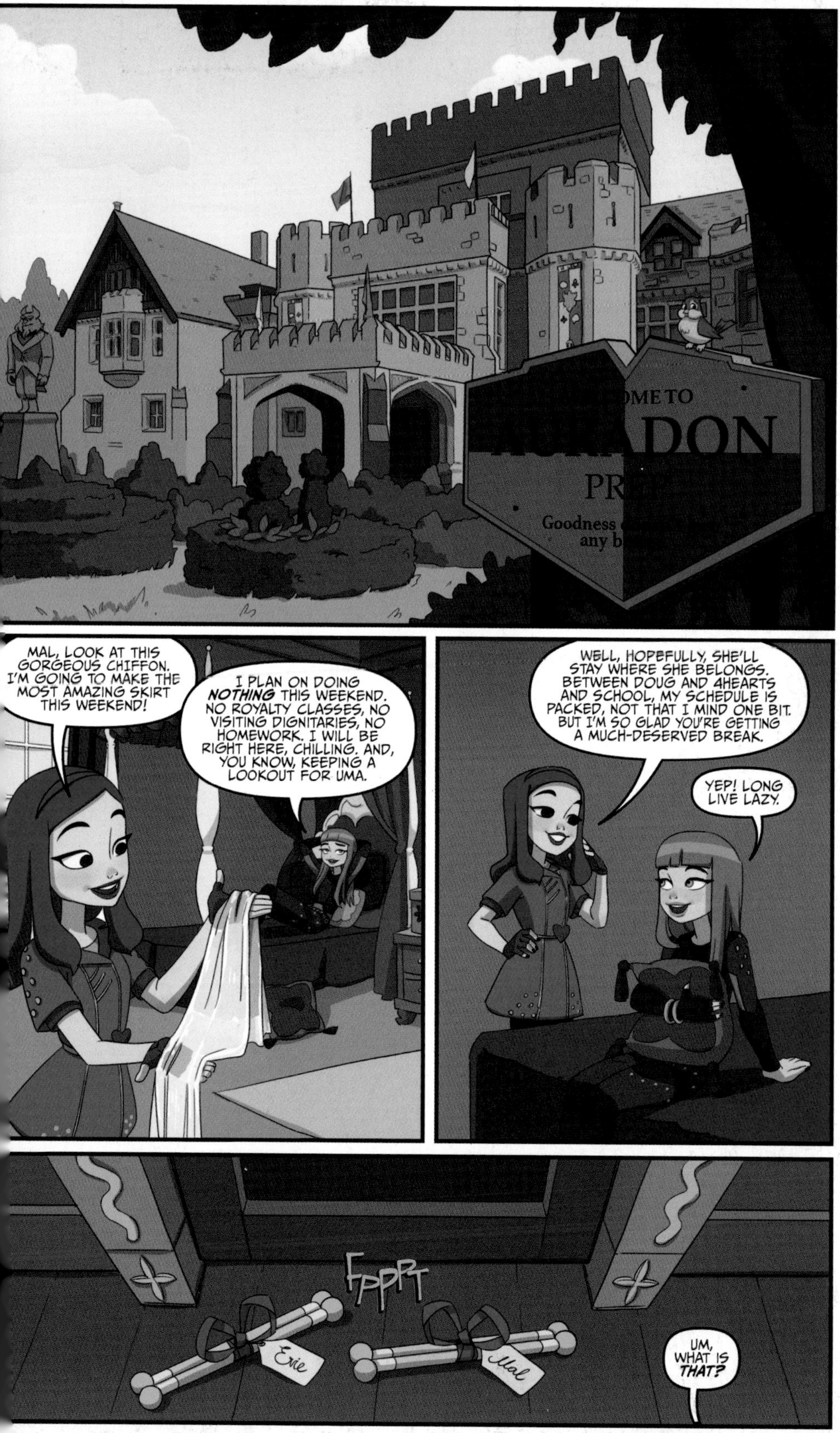
MAL, LOOK AT THIS GORGEOUS CHIFFON. I'M GOING TO MAKE THE MOST AMAZING SKIRT THIS WEEKEND!
I PLAN ON DOING ***NOTHING*** THIS WEEKEND. NO ROYALTY CLASSES, NO VISITING DIGNITARIES, NO HOMEWORK. I WILL BE RIGHT HERE, CHILLING. AND, YOU KNOW, KEEPING A LOOKOUT FOR UMA.
WELL, HOPEFULLY, SHE'LL STAY WHERE SHE BELONGS. BETWEEN DOUG AND 4HEARTS AND SCHOOL, MY SCHEDULE IS PACKED, NOT THAT I MIND ONE BIT. BUT I'M SO GLAD YOU'RE GETTING A MUCH-DESERVED BREAK.
YEP! LONG LIVE LAZY.
FPPPT
Evie
Mal
UM, WHAT IS ***THAT?***

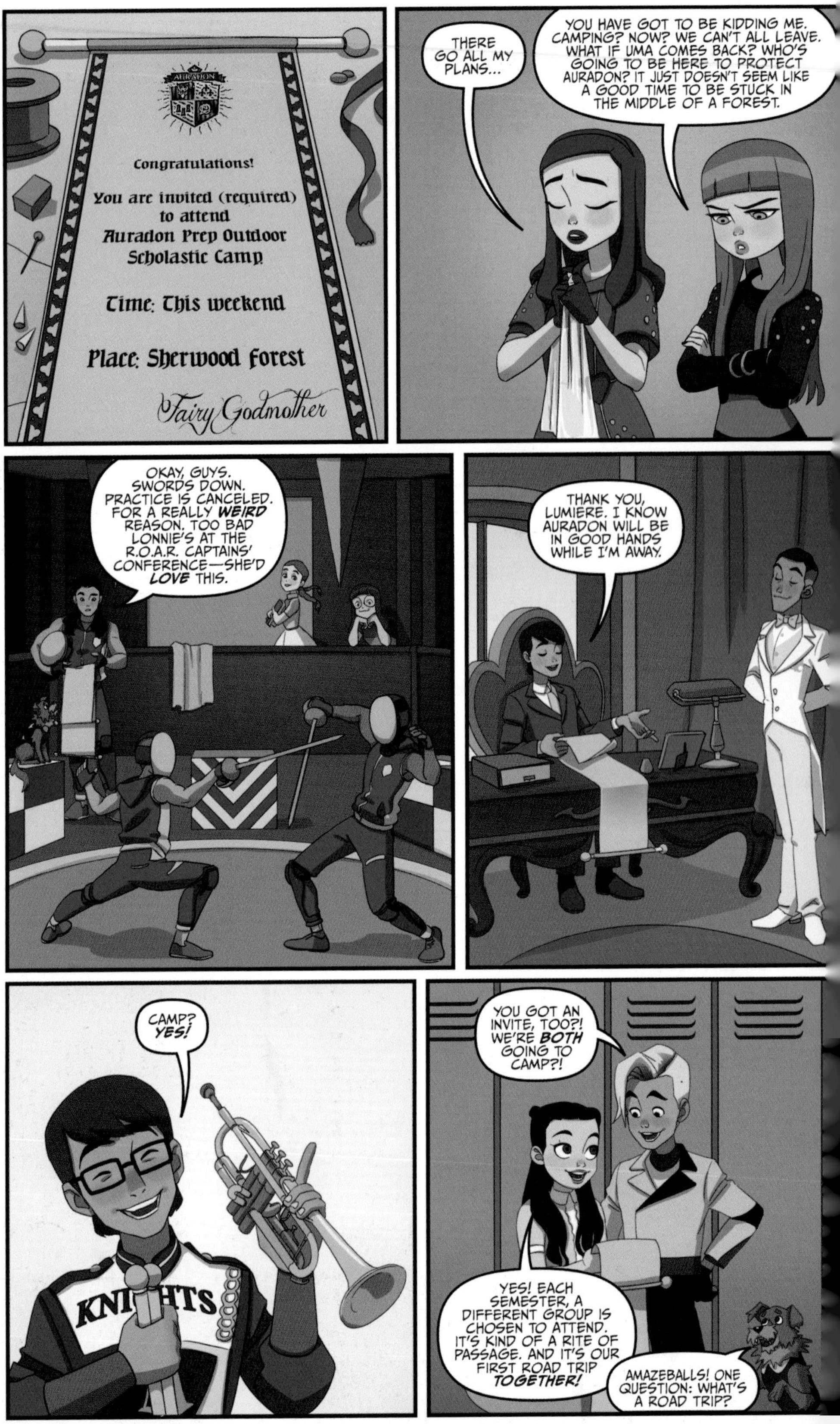
AURADON
Congratulations!
You are invited (required) to attend Auradon Prep Outdoor Scholastic Camp
Time: This weekend
Place: Sherwood Forest
Fairy Godmother
THERE GO ALL MY PLANS...
YOU HAVE GOT TO BE KIDDING ME. CAMPING? NOW? WE CAN'T ALL LEAVE. WHAT IF UMA COMES BACK? WHO'S GOING TO BE HERE TO PROTECT AURADON? IT JUST DOESN'T SEEM LIKE A GOOD TIME TO BE STUCK IN THE MIDDLE OF A FOREST.
OKAY, GUYS. SWORDS DOWN. PRACTICE IS CANCELED. FOR A REALLY WEIRD REASON. TOO BAD LONNIE'S AT THE R.O.A.R. CAPTAINS' CONFERENCE—SHE'D LOVE THIS.
THANK YOU, LUMIERE. I KNOW AURADON WILL BE IN GOOD HANDS WHILE I'M AWAY.
CAMP? YES!
KNIGHTS
YOU GOT AN INVITE, TOO?! WE'RE BOTH GOING TO CAMP?!
YES! EACH SEMESTER, A DIFFERENT GROUP IS CHOSEN TO ATTEND. IT'S KIND OF A RITE OF PASSAGE. AND IT'S OUR FIRST ROAD TRIP TOGETHER!
AMAZEBALLS! ONE QUESTION: WHAT'S A ROAD TRIP?

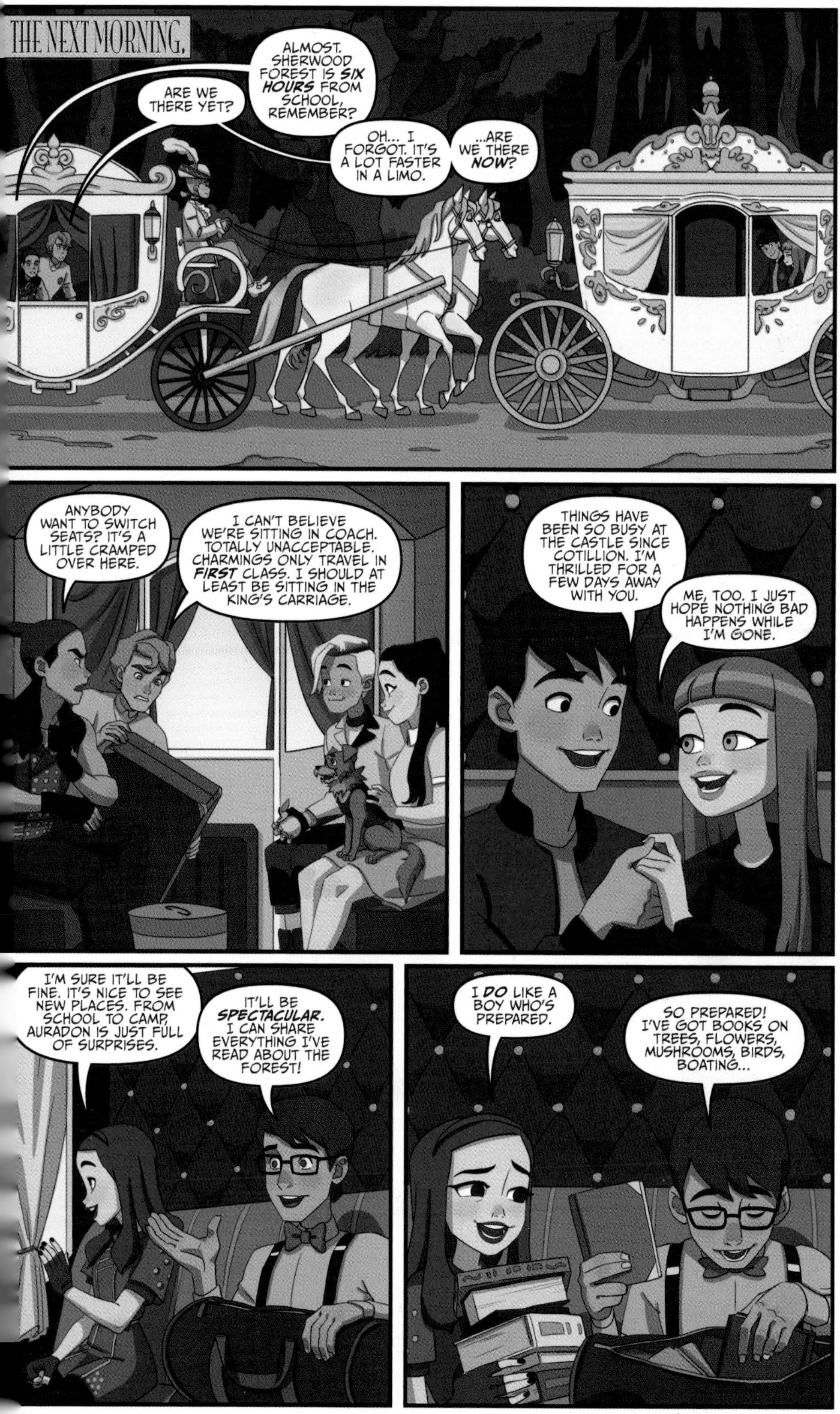
THE NEXT MORNING.
ARE WE THERE YET?
ALMOST. SHERWOOD FOREST IS SIX HOURS FROM SCHOOL, REMEMBER?
OH... I FORGOT. IT'S A LOT FASTER IN A LIMO.
...ARE WE THERE NOW?
ANYBODY WANT TO SWITCH SEATS? IT'S A LITTLE CRAMPED OVER HERE.
I CAN'T BELIEVE WE'RE SITTING IN COACH. TOTALLY UNACCEPTABLE. CHARMINGS ONLY TRAVEL IN FIRST CLASS. I SHOULD AT LEAST BE SITTING IN THE KING'S CARRIAGE.
THINGS HAVE BEEN SO BUSY AT THE CASTLE SINCE COTILLION. I'M THRILLED FOR A FEW DAYS AWAY WITH YOU.
ME, TOO. I JUST HOPE NOTHING BAD HAPPENS WHILE I'M GONE.
I'M SURE IT'LL BE FINE. IT'S NICE TO SEE NEW PLACES. FROM SCHOOL TO CAMP, AURADON IS JUST FULL OF SURPRISES.
IT'LL BE SPECTACULAR. I CAN SHARE EVERYTHING I'VE READ ABOUT THE FOREST!
I DO LIKE A BOY WHO'S PREPARED.
SO PREPARED! I'VE GOT BOOKS ON TREES, FLOWERS, MUSHROOMS, BIRDS, BOATING...

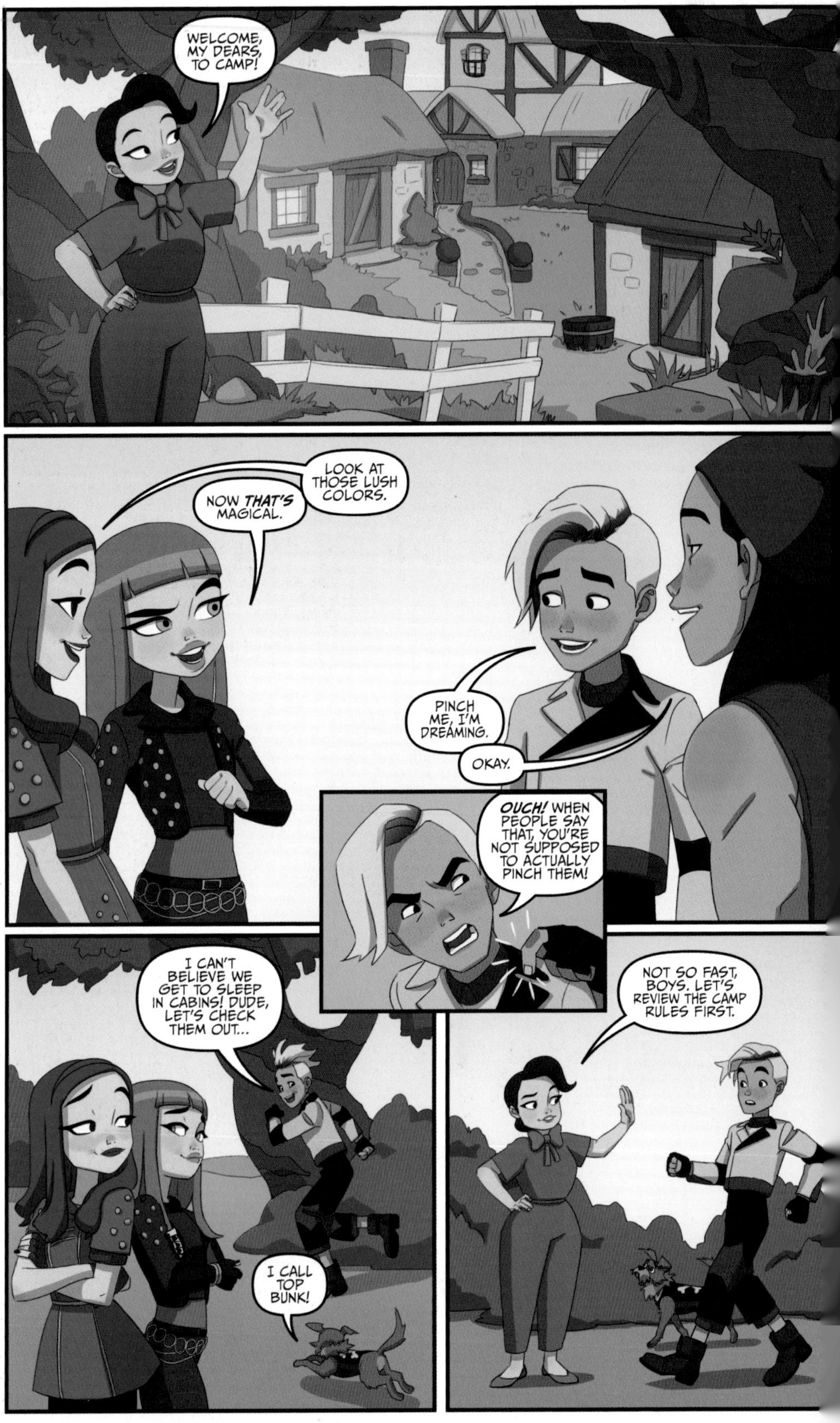
WELCOME, MY DEARS, TO CAMP!
LOOK AT THOSE LUSH COLORS.
NOW THAT'S MAGICAL.
PINCH ME, I'M DREAMING.
OKAY.
OUCH! WHEN PEOPLE SAY THAT, YOU'RE NOT SUPPOSED TO ACTUALLY PINCH THEM!
I CAN'T BELIEVE WE GET TO SLEEP IN CABINS! DUDE, LET'S CHECK THEM OUT...
I CALL TOP BUNK!
NOT SO FAST, BOYS. LET'S REVIEW THE CAMP RULES FIRST.

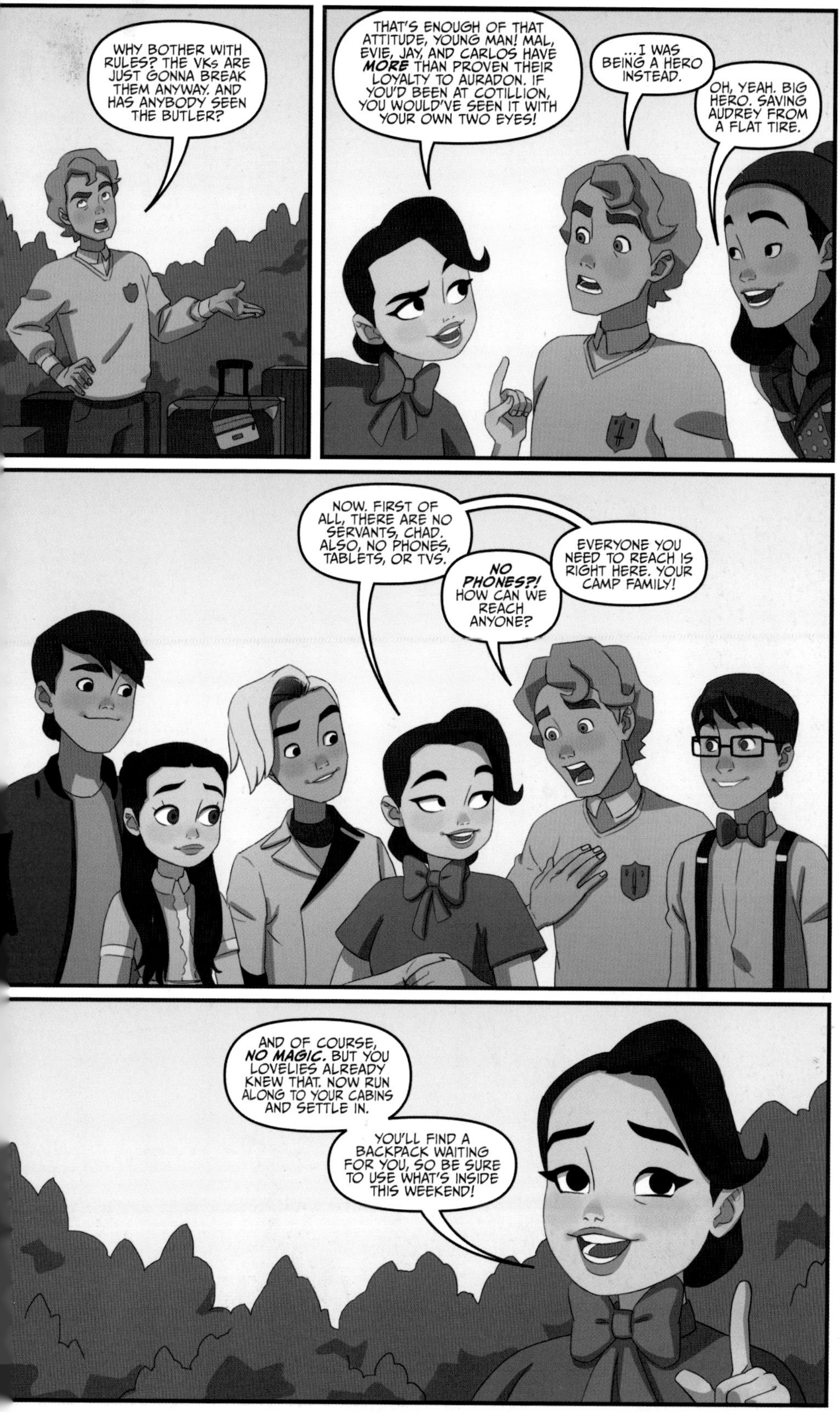
WHY BOTHER WITH RULES? THE VKs ARE JUST GONNA BREAK THEM ANYWAY. AND HAS ANYBODY SEEN THE BUTLER?
THAT'S ENOUGH OF THAT ATTITUDE, YOUNG MAN! MAL, EVIE, JAY, AND CARLOS HAVE MORE THAN PROVEN THEIR LOYALTY TO AURADON. IF YOU'D BEEN AT COTILLION, YOU WOULD'VE SEEN IT WITH YOUR OWN TWO EYES!
...I WAS BEING A HERO INSTEAD.
OH, YEAH. BIG HERO. SAVING AUDREY FROM A FLAT TIRE.
NOW. FIRST OF ALL, THERE ARE NO SERVANTS, CHAD. ALSO, NO PHONES, TABLETS, OR TVS.
NO PHONES?! HOW CAN WE REACH ANYONE?
EVERYONE YOU NEED TO REACH IS RIGHT HERE. YOUR CAMP FAMILY!
AND OF COURSE, NO MAGIC. BUT YOU LOVELIES ALREADY KNEW THAT. NOW RUN ALONG TO YOUR CABINS AND SETTLE IN.
YOU'LL FIND A BACKPACK WAITING FOR YOU, SO BE SURE TO USE WHAT'S INSIDE THIS WEEKEND!

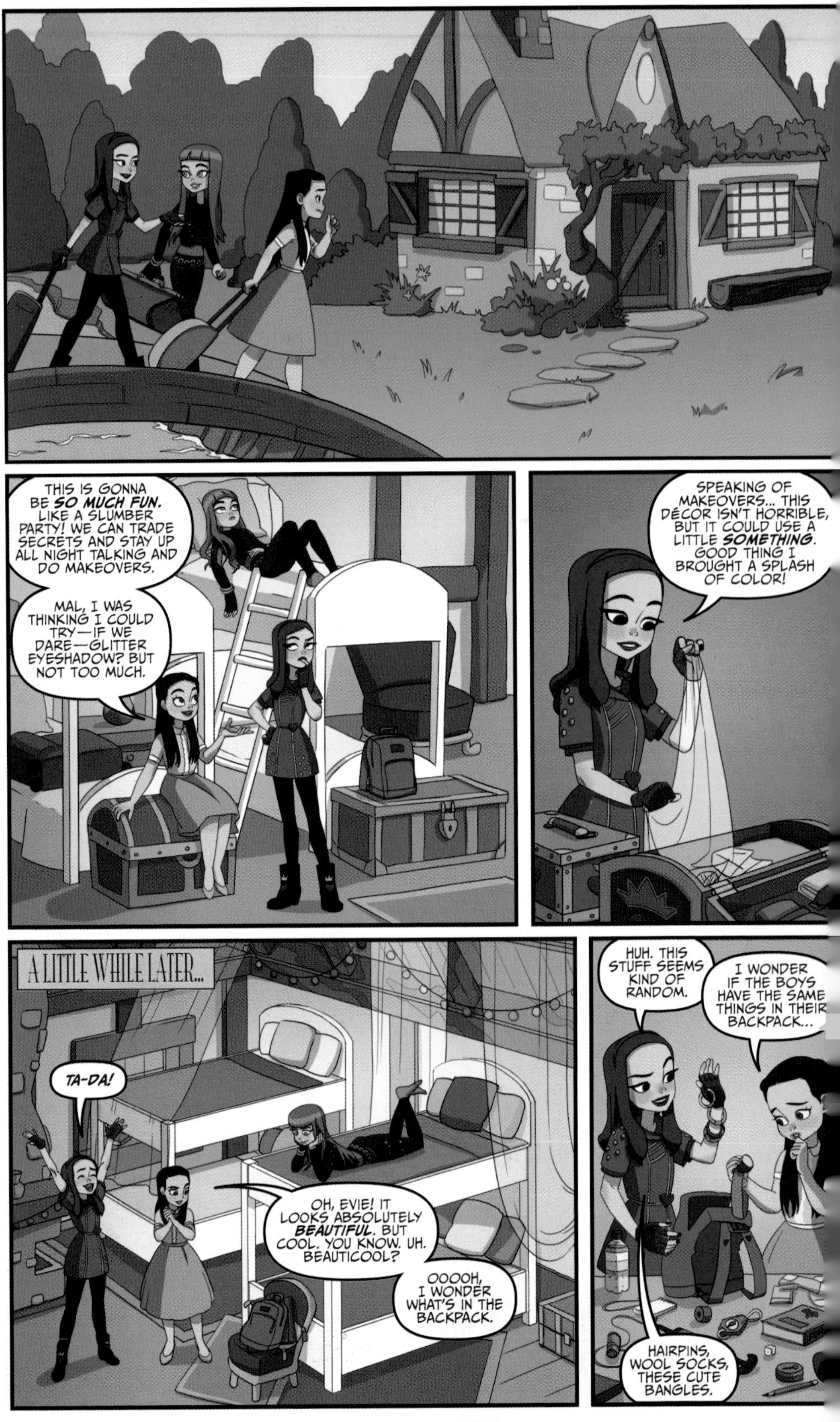

THIS IS GONNA BE SO MUCH FUN. LIKE A SLUMBER PARTY! WE CAN TRADE SECRETS AND STAY UP ALL NIGHT TALKING AND DO MAKEOVERS.
MAL, I WAS THINKING I COULD TRY—IF WE DARE—GLITTER EYESHADOW? BUT NOT TOO MUCH.
SPEAKING OF MAKEOVERS... THIS DÉCOR ISN'T HORRIBLE, BUT IT COULD USE A LITTLE SOMETHING. GOOD THING I BROUGHT A SPLASH OF COLOR!
A LITTLE WHILE LATER...
TA-DA!
OH, EVIE! IT LOOKS ABSOLUTELY BEAUTIFUL. BUT COOL. YOU KNOW. UH. BEAUTICOOL?
OOOOH, I WONDER WHAT'S IN THE BACKPACK.
HUH. THIS STUFF SEEMS KIND OF RANDOM.
I WONDER IF THE BOYS HAVE THE SAME THINGS IN THEIR BACKPACK...
HAIRPINS, WOOL SOCKS, THESE CUTE BANGLES.

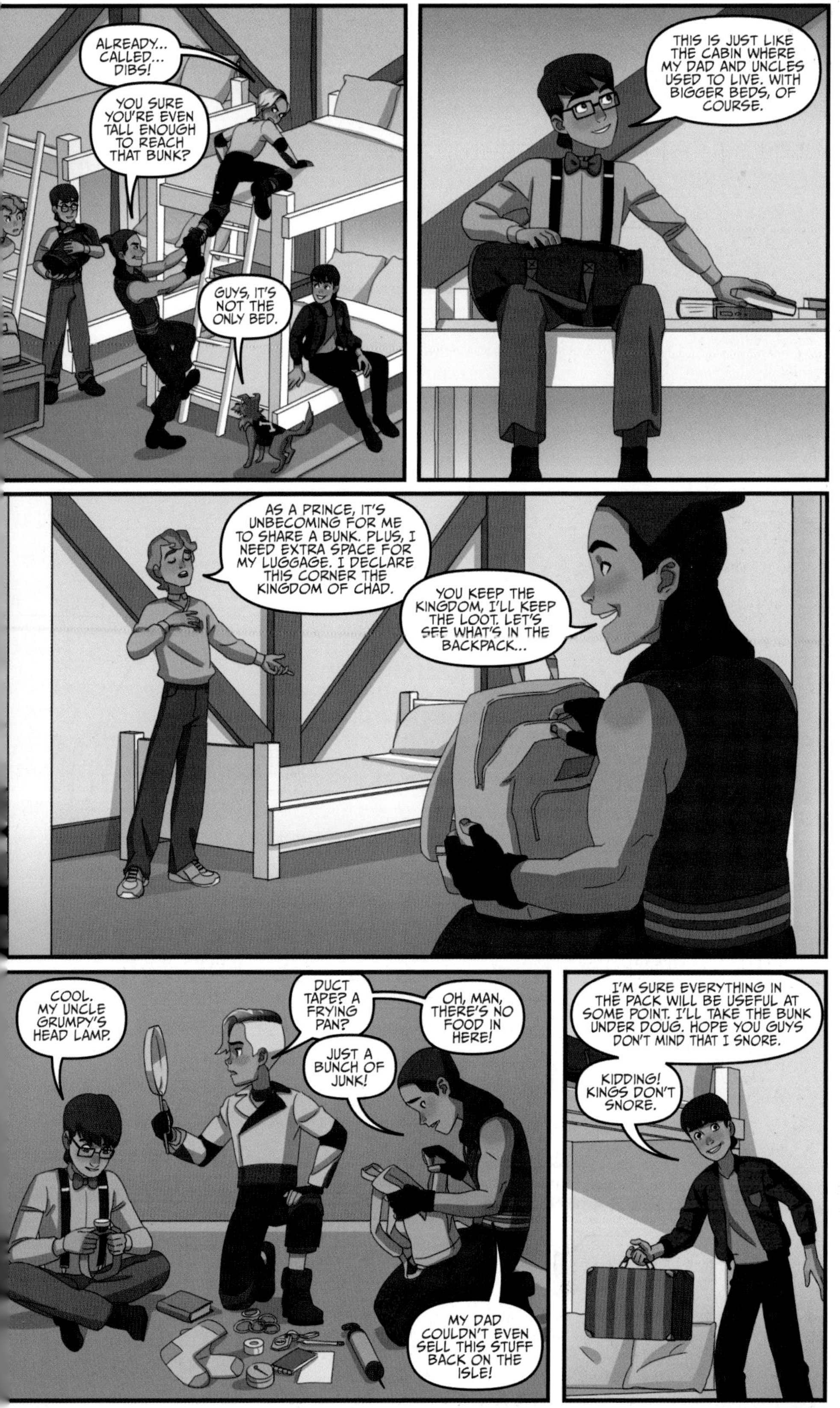
ALREADY... CALLED... DIBS!
YOU SURE YOU'RE EVEN TALL ENOUGH TO REACH THAT BUNK?
GUYS, IT'S NOT THE ONLY BED.
THIS IS JUST LIKE THE CABIN WHERE MY DAD AND UNCLES USED TO LIVE. WITH BIGGER BEDS, OF COURSE.
AS A PRINCE, IT'S UNBECOMING FOR ME TO SHARE A BUNK. PLUS, I NEED EXTRA SPACE FOR MY LUGGAGE. I DECLARE THIS CORNER THE KINGDOM OF CHAD.
YOU KEEP THE KINGDOM, I'LL KEEP THE LOOT. LET'S SEE WHAT'S IN THE BACKPACK...
COOL. MY UNCLE GRUMPY'S HEAD LAMP.
DUCT TAPE? A FRYING PAN?
JUST A BUNCH OF JUNK!
OH, MAN, THERE'S NO FOOD IN HERE!
MY DAD COULDN'T EVEN SELL THIS STUFF BACK ON THE ISLE!
I'M SURE EVERYTHING IN THE PACK WILL BE USEFUL AT SOME POINT. I'LL TAKE THE BUNK UNDER DOUG. HOPE YOU GUYS DON'T MIND THAT I SNORE.
KIDDING! KINGS DON'T SNORE.

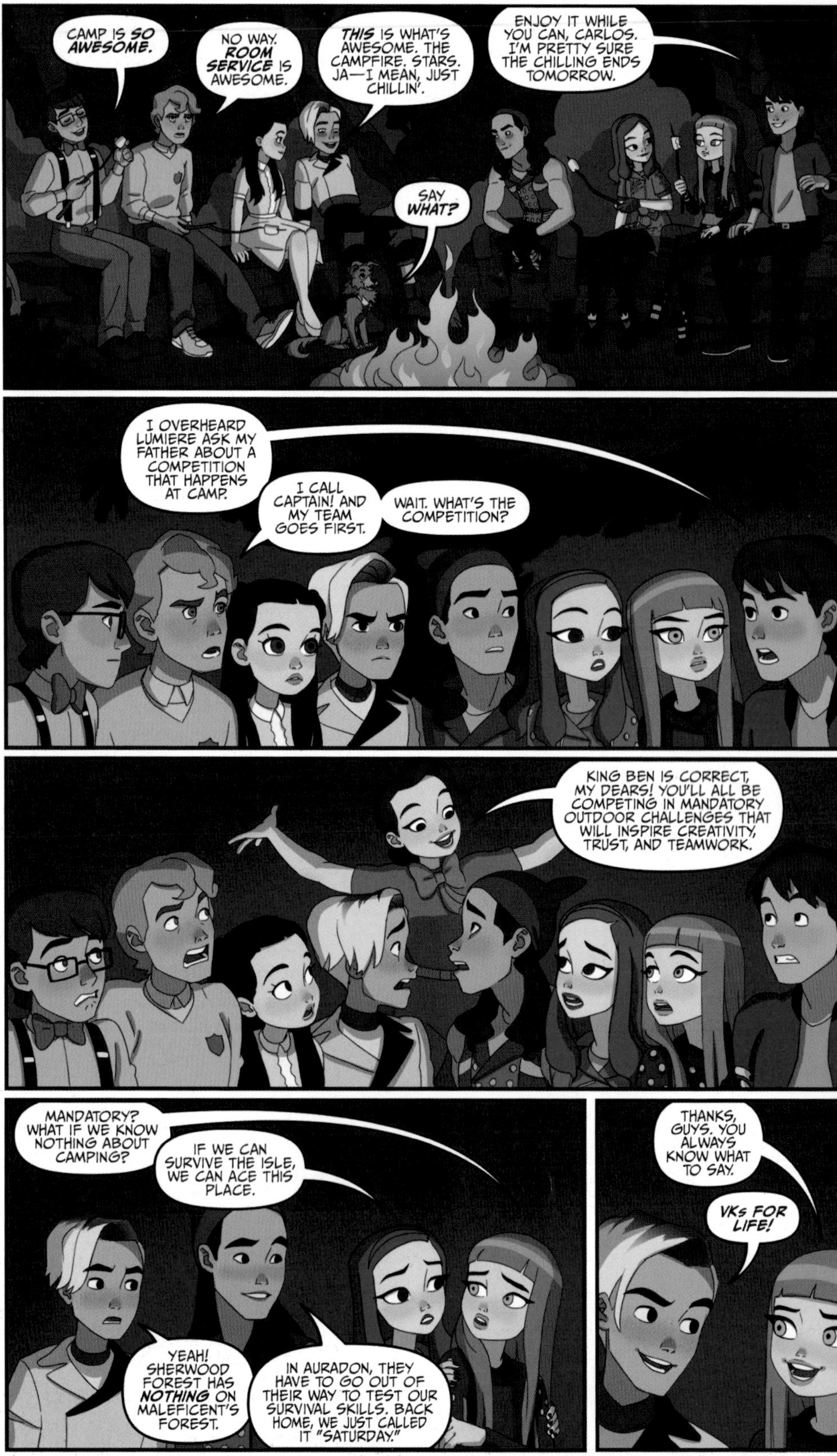

CAMP IS **SO AWESOME.**
NO WAY. **ROOM SERVICE** IS AWESOME.
THIS IS WHAT'S AWESOME. THE CAMPFIRE. STARS. JA—I MEAN, JUST CHILLIN'.
SAY **WHAT?**
ENJOY IT WHILE YOU CAN, CARLOS. I'M PRETTY SURE THE CHILLING ENDS TOMORROW.
I OVERHEARD LUMIERE ASK MY FATHER ABOUT A COMPETITION THAT HAPPENS AT CAMP.
I CALL CAPTAIN! AND MY TEAM GOES FIRST.
WAIT. WHAT'S THE COMPETITION?
KING BEN IS CORRECT, MY DEARS! YOU'LL ALL BE COMPETING IN MANDATORY OUTDOOR CHALLENGES THAT WILL INSPIRE CREATIVITY, TRUST, AND TEAMWORK.
MANDATORY? WHAT IF WE KNOW NOTHING ABOUT CAMPING?
IF WE CAN SURVIVE THE ISLE, WE CAN ACE THIS PLACE.
YEAH! SHERWOOD FOREST HAS **NOTHING** ON MALEFICENT'S FOREST.
IN AURADON, THEY HAVE TO GO OUT OF THEIR WAY TO TEST OUR SURVIVAL SKILLS. BACK HOME, WE JUST CALLED IT "SATURDAY."
THANKS, GUYS. YOU ALWAYS KNOW WHAT TO SAY.
VKs FOR LIFE!

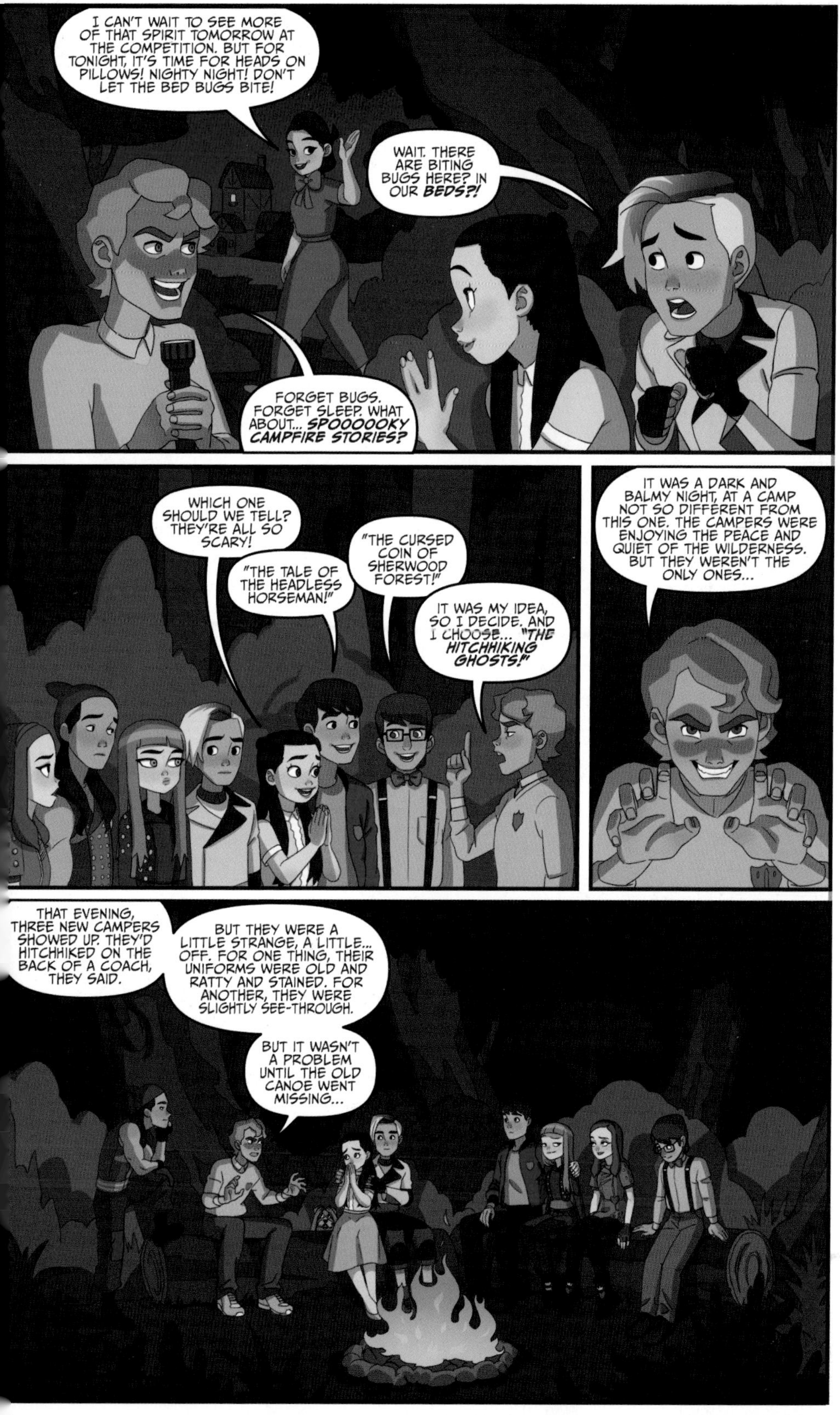
I CAN'T WAIT TO SEE MORE OF THAT SPIRIT TOMORROW AT THE COMPETITION. BUT FOR TONIGHT, IT'S TIME FOR HEADS ON PILLOWS! NIGHTY NIGHT! DON'T LET THE BED BUGS BITE!
WAIT. THERE ARE BITING BUGS HERE? IN OUR BEDS?!
FORGET BUGS. FORGET SLEEP. WHAT ABOUT... SPOOOOOKY CAMPFIRE STORIES?
WHICH ONE SHOULD WE TELL? THEY'RE ALL SO SCARY!
"THE TALE OF THE HEADLESS HORSEMAN!"
"THE CURSED COIN OF SHERWOOD FOREST!"
IT WAS MY IDEA, SO I DECIDE. AND I CHOOSE... "THE HITCHHIKING GHOSTS!"
IT WAS A DARK AND BALMY NIGHT, AT A CAMP NOT SO DIFFERENT FROM THIS ONE. THE CAMPERS WERE ENJOYING THE PEACE AND QUIET OF THE WILDERNESS. BUT THEY WEREN'T THE ONLY ONES...
THAT EVENING, THREE NEW CAMPERS SHOWED UP. THEY'D HITCHHIKED ON THE BACK OF A COACH, THEY SAID.
BUT THEY WERE A LITTLE STRANGE, A LITTLE... OFF. FOR ONE THING, THEIR UNIFORMS WERE OLD AND RATTY AND STAINED. FOR ANOTHER, THEY WERE SLIGHTLY SEE-THROUGH.
BUT IT WASN'T A PROBLEM UNTIL THE OLD CANOE WENT MISSING...

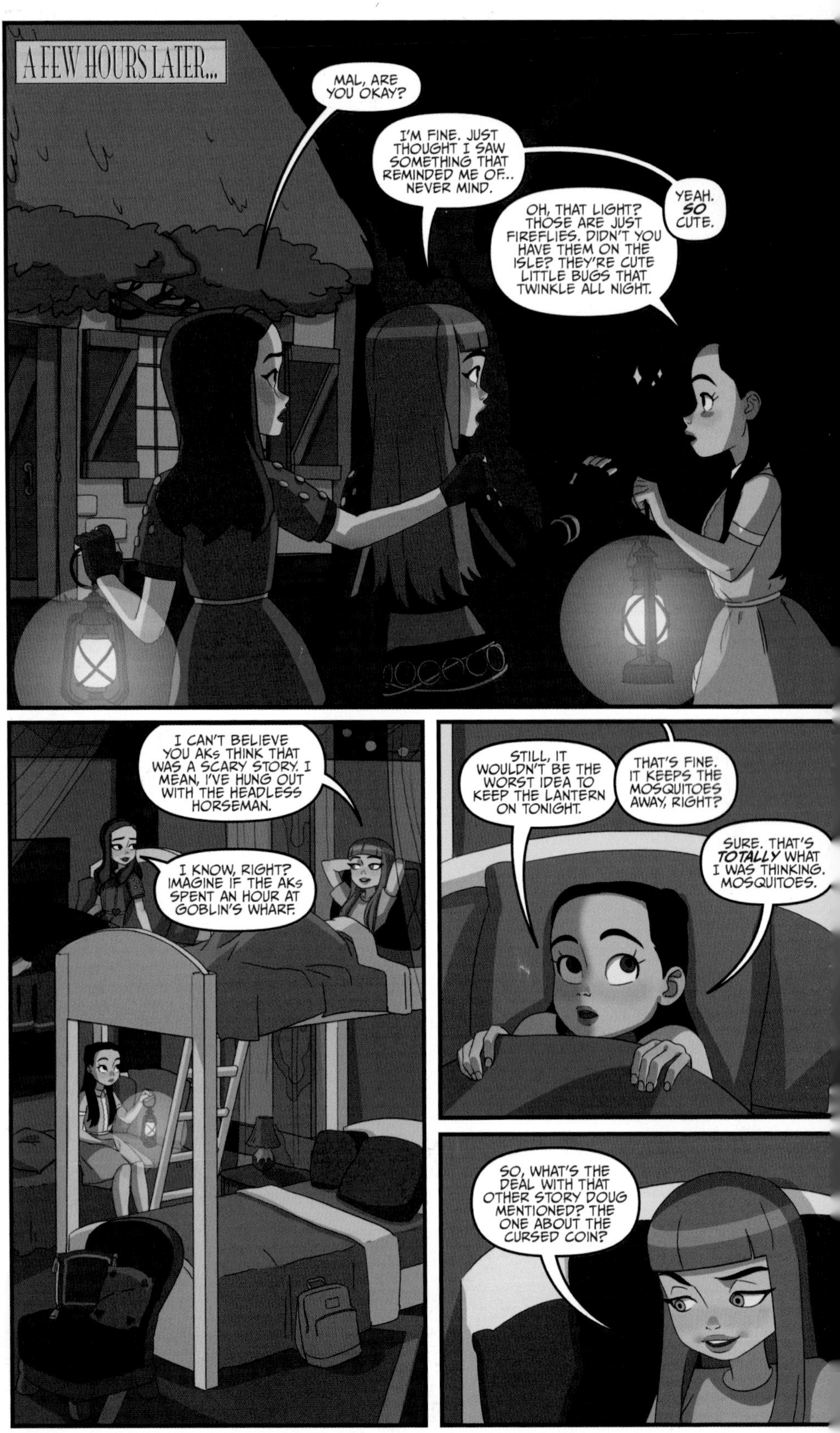
A FEW HOURS LATER...
MAL, ARE YOU OKAY?
I'M FINE. JUST THOUGHT I SAW SOMETHING THAT REMINDED ME OF... NEVER MIND.
OH, THAT LIGHT? THOSE ARE JUST FIREFLIES. DIDN'T YOU HAVE THEM ON THE ISLE? THEY'RE CUTE LITTLE BUGS THAT TWINKLE ALL NIGHT.
YEAH. SO CUTE.
I CAN'T BELIEVE YOU AKs THINK THAT WAS A SCARY STORY. I MEAN, I'VE HUNG OUT WITH THE HEADLESS HORSEMAN.
I KNOW, RIGHT? IMAGINE IF THE AKs SPENT AN HOUR AT GOBLIN'S WHARF.
STILL, IT WOULDN'T BE THE WORST IDEA TO KEEP THE LANTERN ON TONIGHT.
THAT'S FINE. IT KEEPS THE MOSQUITOES AWAY, RIGHT?
SURE. THAT'S TOTALLY WHAT I WAS THINKING. MOSQUITOES.
SO, WHAT'S THE DEAL WITH THAT OTHER STORY DOUG MENTIONED? THE ONE ABOUT THE CURSED COIN?

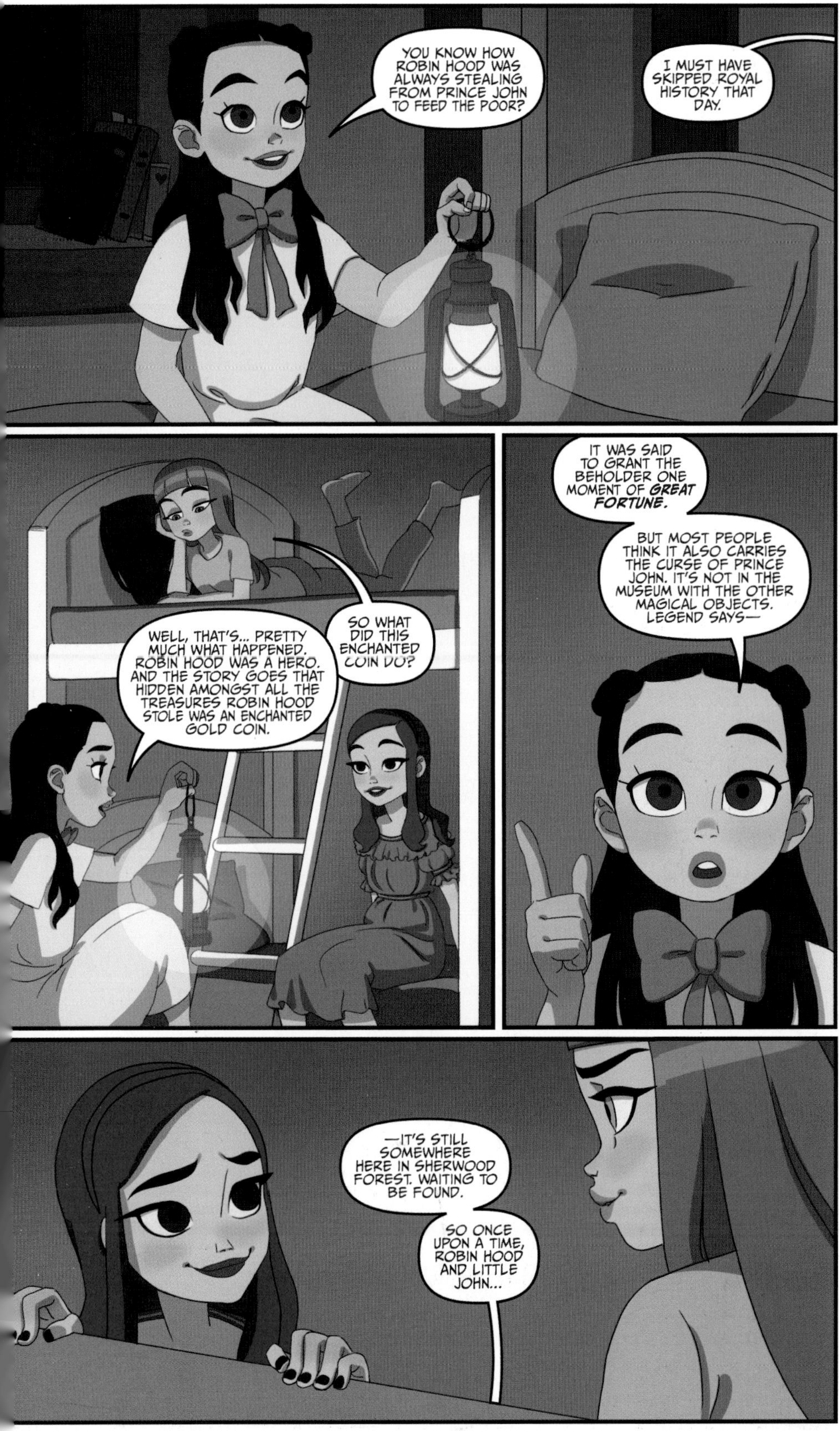
YOU KNOW HOW ROBIN HOOD WAS ALWAYS STEALING FROM PRINCE JOHN TO FEED THE POOR?
I MUST HAVE SKIPPED ROYAL HISTORY THAT DAY.
WELL, THAT'S... PRETTY MUCH WHAT HAPPENED. ROBIN HOOD WAS A HERO. AND THE STORY GOES THAT HIDDEN AMONGST ALL THE TREASURES ROBIN HOOD STOLE WAS AN ENCHANTED GOLD COIN.
SO WHAT DID THIS ENCHANTED COIN DO?
IT WAS SAID TO GRANT THE BEHOLDER ONE MOMENT OF GREAT FORTUNE.
BUT MOST PEOPLE THINK IT ALSO CARRIES THE CURSE OF PRINCE JOHN. IT'S NOT IN THE MUSEUM WITH THE OTHER MAGICAL OBJECTS. LEGEND SAYS—
—IT'S STILL SOMEWHERE HERE IN SHERWOOD FOREST. WAITING TO BE FOUND.
SO ONCE UPON A TIME, ROBIN HOOD AND LITTLE JOHN...

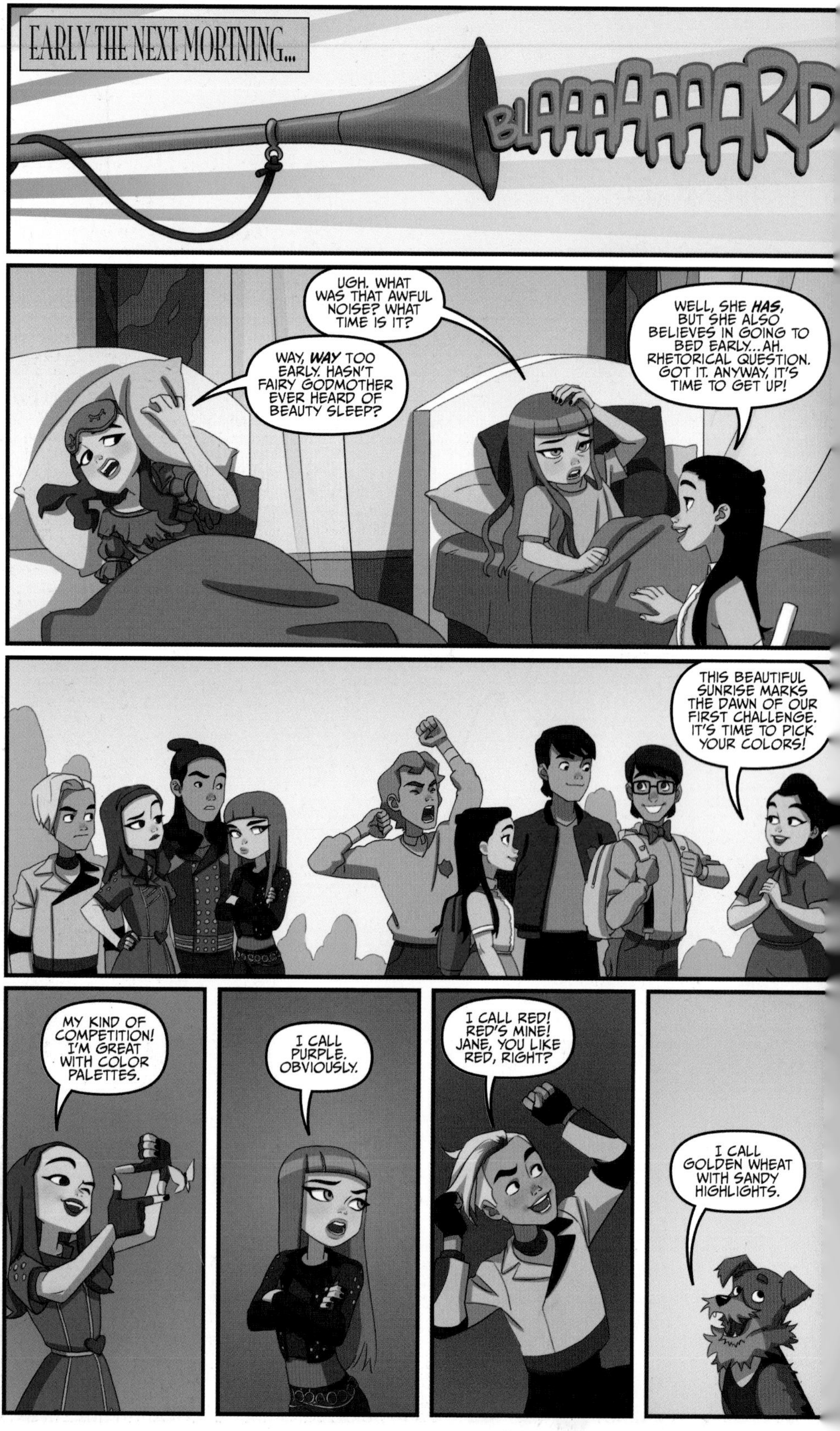
EARLY THE NEXT MORTNING...
BLAAAAAAARD
UGH. WHAT WAS THAT AWFUL NOISE? WHAT TIME IS IT?
WAY, WAY TOO EARLY. HASN'T FAIRY GODMOTHER EVER HEARD OF BEAUTY SLEEP?
WELL, SHE HAS, BUT SHE ALSO BELIEVES IN GOING TO BED EARLY...AH. RHETORICAL QUESTION. GOT IT. ANYWAY, IT'S TIME TO GET UP!
THIS BEAUTIFUL SUNRISE MARKS THE DAWN OF OUR FIRST CHALLENGE. IT'S TIME TO PICK YOUR COLORS!
MY KIND OF COMPETITION! I'M GREAT WITH COLOR PALETTES.
I CALL PURPLE. OBVIOUSLY.
I CALL RED! RED'S MINE! JANE, YOU LIKE RED, RIGHT?
I CALL GOLDEN WHEAT WITH SANDY HIGHLIGHTS.

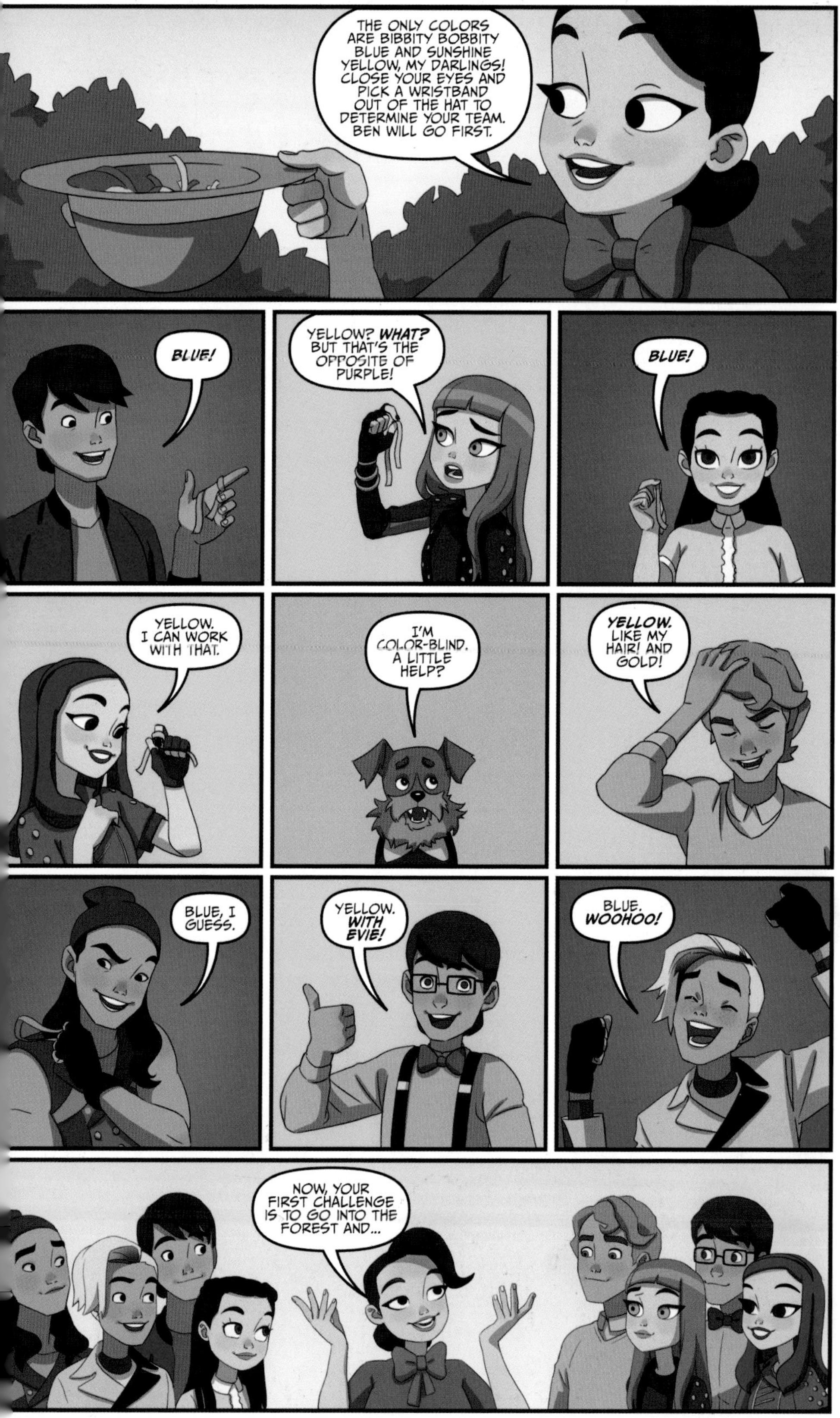
THE ONLY COLORS ARE BIBBITY BOBBITY BLUE AND SUNSHINE YELLOW, MY DARLINGS! CLOSE YOUR EYES AND PICK A WRISTBAND OUT OF THE HAT TO DETERMINE YOUR TEAM. BEN WILL GO FIRST.
BLUE!
YELLOW? WHAT? BUT THAT'S THE OPPOSITE OF PURPLE!
BLUE!
YELLOW. I CAN WORK WITH THAT.
I'M COLOR-BLIND. A LITTLE HELP?
YELLOW. LIKE MY HAIR! AND GOLD!
BLUE, I GUESS.
YELLOW. WITH EVIE!
BLUE. WOOHOO!
NOW, YOUR FIRST CHALLENGE IS TO GO INTO THE FOREST AND...

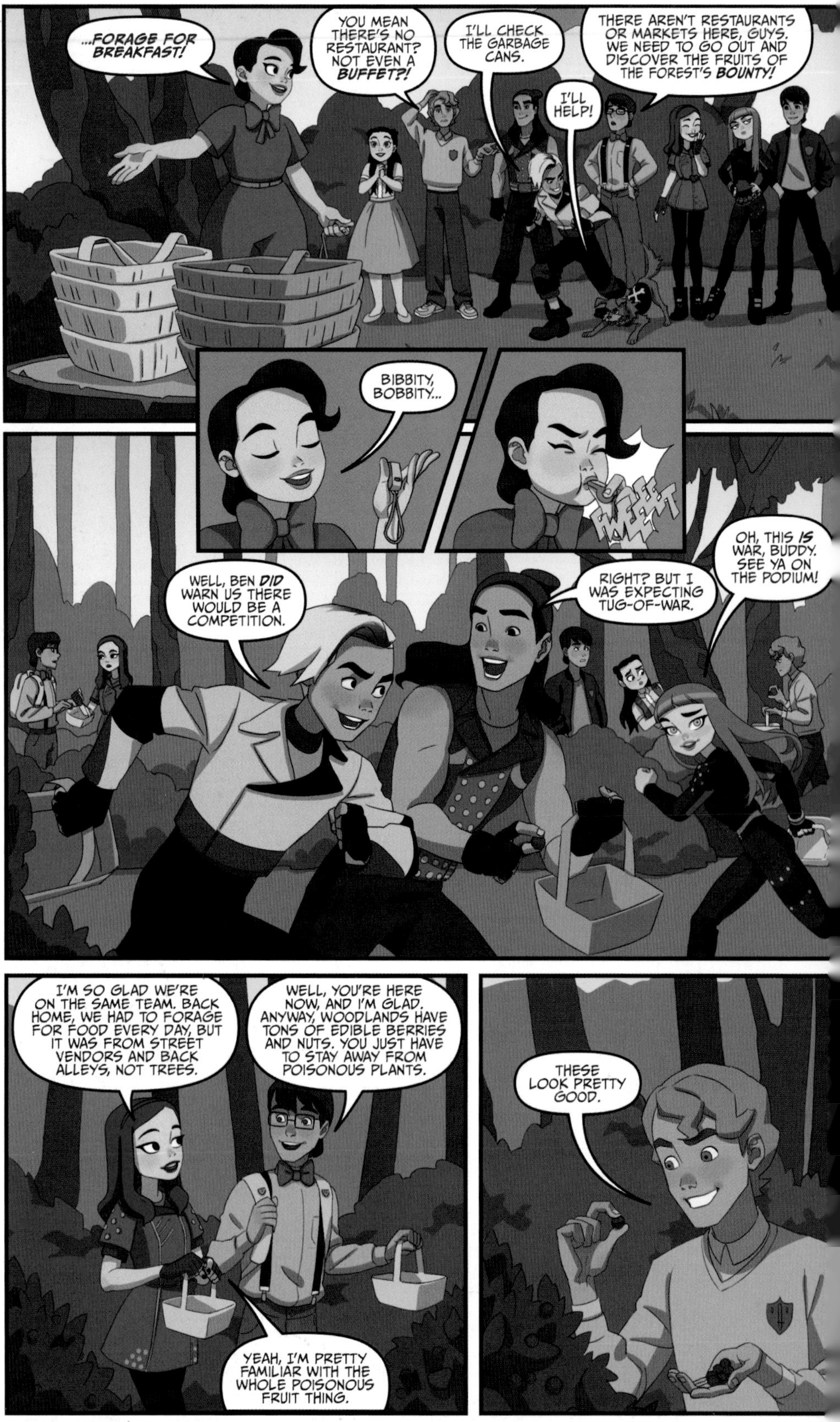

...FORAGE FOR BREAKFAST!
YOU MEAN THERE'S NO RESTAURANT? NOT EVEN A BUFFET?!
I'LL CHECK THE GARBAGE CANS.
I'LL HELP!
THERE AREN'T RESTAURANTS OR MARKETS HERE, GUYS. WE NEED TO GO OUT AND DISCOVER THE FRUITS OF THE FOREST'S BOUNTY!
BIBBITY, BOBBITY...
FWEEEET
WELL, BEN DID WARN US THERE WOULD BE A COMPETITION.
RIGHT? BUT I WAS EXPECTING TUG-OF-WAR.
OH, THIS IS WAR, BUDDY. SEE YA ON THE PODIUM!
I'M SO GLAD WE'RE ON THE SAME TEAM. BACK HOME, WE HAD TO FORAGE FOR FOOD EVERY DAY, BUT IT WAS FROM STREET VENDORS AND BACK ALLEYS, NOT TREES.
WELL, YOU'RE HERE NOW, AND I'M GLAD. ANYWAY, WOODLANDS HAVE TONS OF EDIBLE BERRIES AND NUTS. YOU JUST HAVE TO STAY AWAY FROM POISONOUS PLANTS.
YEAH, I'M PRETTY FAMILIAR WITH THE WHOLE POISONOUS FRUIT THING.
THESE LOOK PRETTY GOOD.

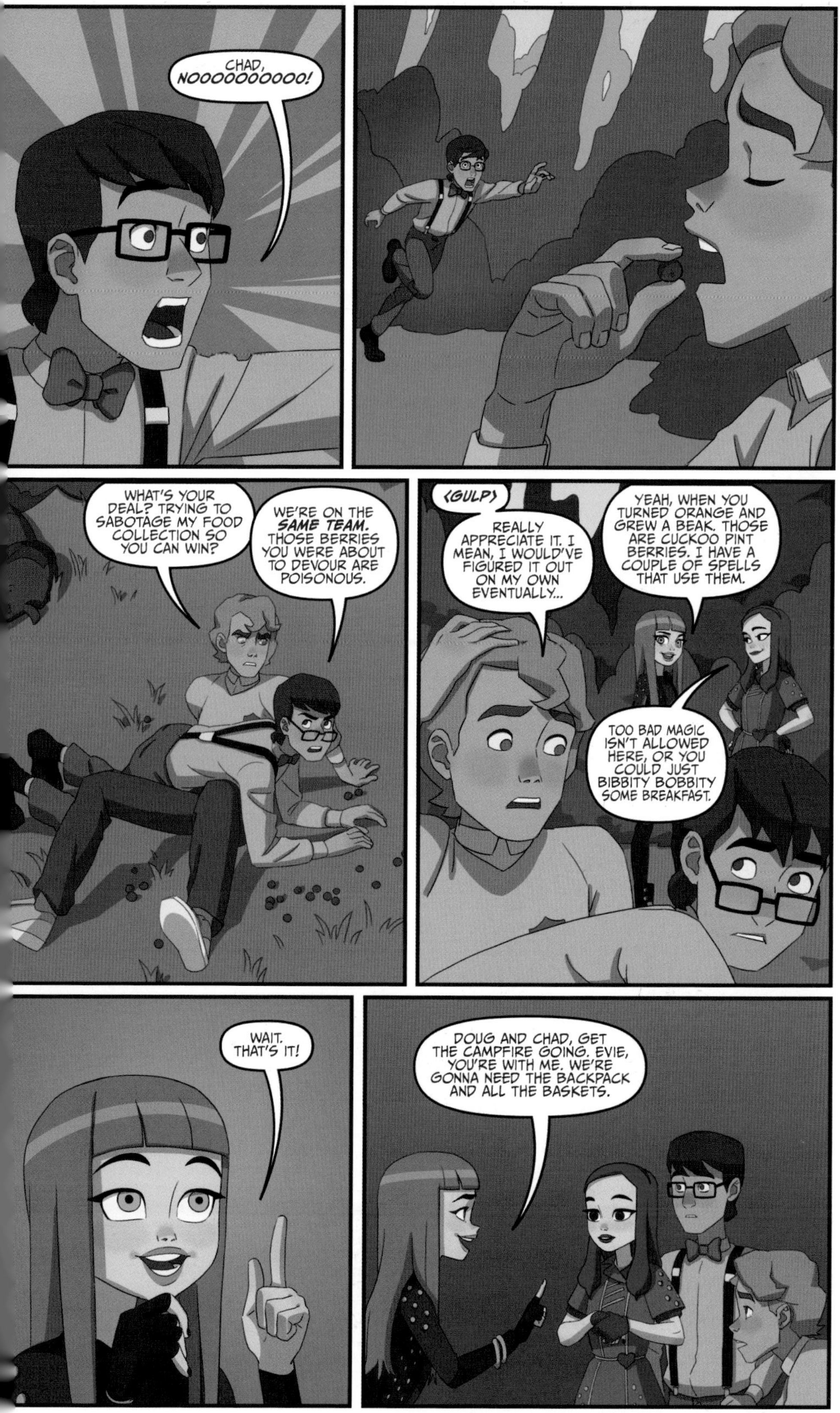
CHAD, NOOOOOOOOOO!
WHAT'S YOUR DEAL? TRYING TO SABOTAGE MY FOOD COLLECTION SO YOU CAN WIN?
WE'RE ON THE **SAME TEAM.** THOSE BERRIES YOU WERE ABOUT TO DEVOUR ARE POISONOUS.
<GULP>
REALLY APPRECIATE IT. I MEAN, I WOULD'VE FIGURED IT OUT ON MY OWN EVENTUALLY...
YEAH, WHEN YOU TURNED ORANGE AND GREW A BEAK. THOSE ARE CUCKOO PINT BERRIES. I HAVE A COUPLE OF SPELLS THAT USE THEM.
TOO BAD MAGIC ISN'T ALLOWED HERE, OR YOU COULD JUST BIBBITY BOBBITY SOME BREAKFAST.
WAIT. THAT'S IT!
DOUG AND CHAD, GET THE CAMPFIRE GOING. EVIE, YOU'RE WITH ME. WE'RE GONNA NEED THE BACKPACK AND ALL THE BASKETS.

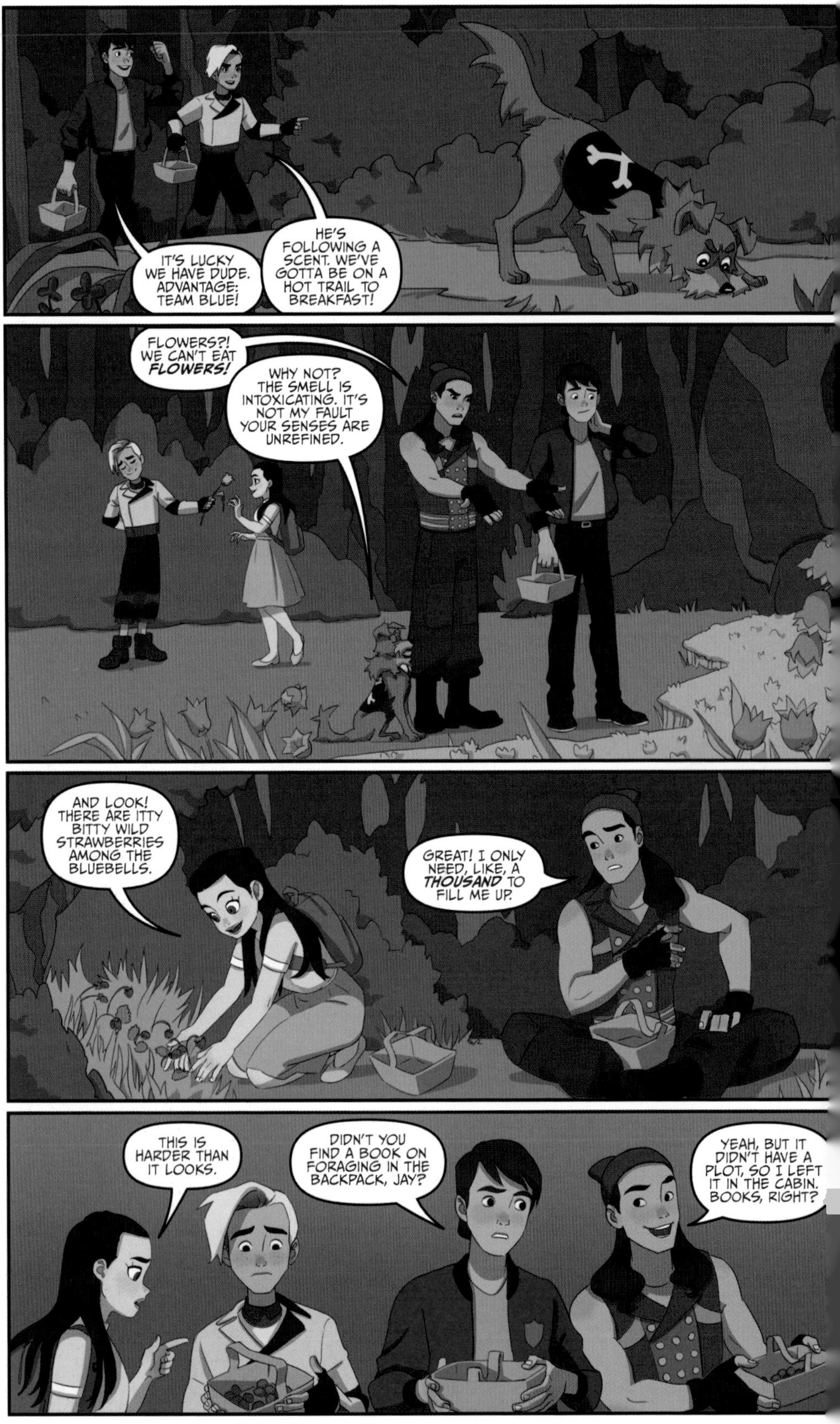
IT'S LUCKY WE HAVE DUDE. ADVANTAGE: TEAM BLUE!
HE'S FOLLOWING A SCENT. WE'VE GOTTA BE ON A HOT TRAIL TO BREAKFAST!
FLOWERS?! WE CAN'T EAT *FLOWERS!*
WHY NOT? THE SMELL IS INTOXICATING. IT'S NOT MY FAULT YOUR SENSES ARE UNREFINED.
AND LOOK! THERE ARE ITTY BITTY WILD STRAWBERRIES AMONG THE BLUEBELLS.
GREAT! I ONLY NEED, LIKE, A *THOUSAND* TO FILL ME UP.
THIS IS HARDER THAN IT LOOKS.
DIDN'T YOU FIND A BOOK ON FORAGING IN THE BACKPACK, JAY?
YEAH, BUT IT DIDN'T HAVE A PLOT, SO I LEFT IT IN THE CABIN. BOOKS, RIGHT?

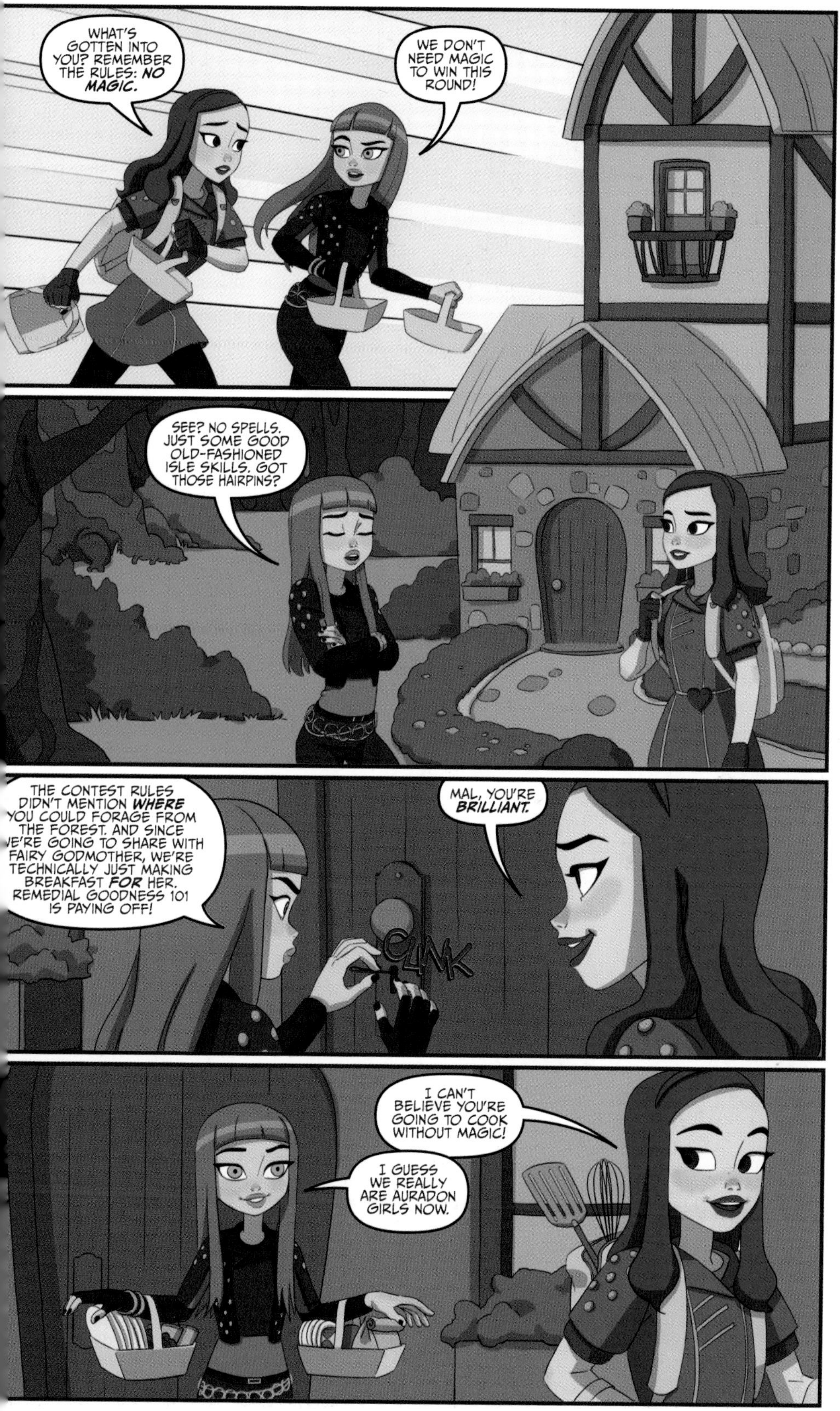

WHAT'S GOTTEN INTO YOU? REMEMBER THE RULES: NO MAGIC.
WE DON'T NEED MAGIC TO WIN THIS ROUND!
SEE? NO SPELLS. JUST SOME GOOD OLD-FASHIONED ISLE SKILLS. GOT THOSE HAIRPINS?
THE CONTEST RULES DIDN'T MENTION WHERE YOU COULD FORAGE FROM THE FOREST. AND SINCE WE'RE GOING TO SHARE WITH FAIRY GODMOTHER, WE'RE TECHNICALLY JUST MAKING BREAKFAST FOR HER. REMEDIAL GOODNESS 101 IS PAYING OFF!
MAL, YOU'RE BRILLIANT.
CLINK
I CAN'T BELIEVE YOU'RE GOING TO COOK WITHOUT MAGIC!
I GUESS WE REALLY ARE AURADON GIRLS NOW.

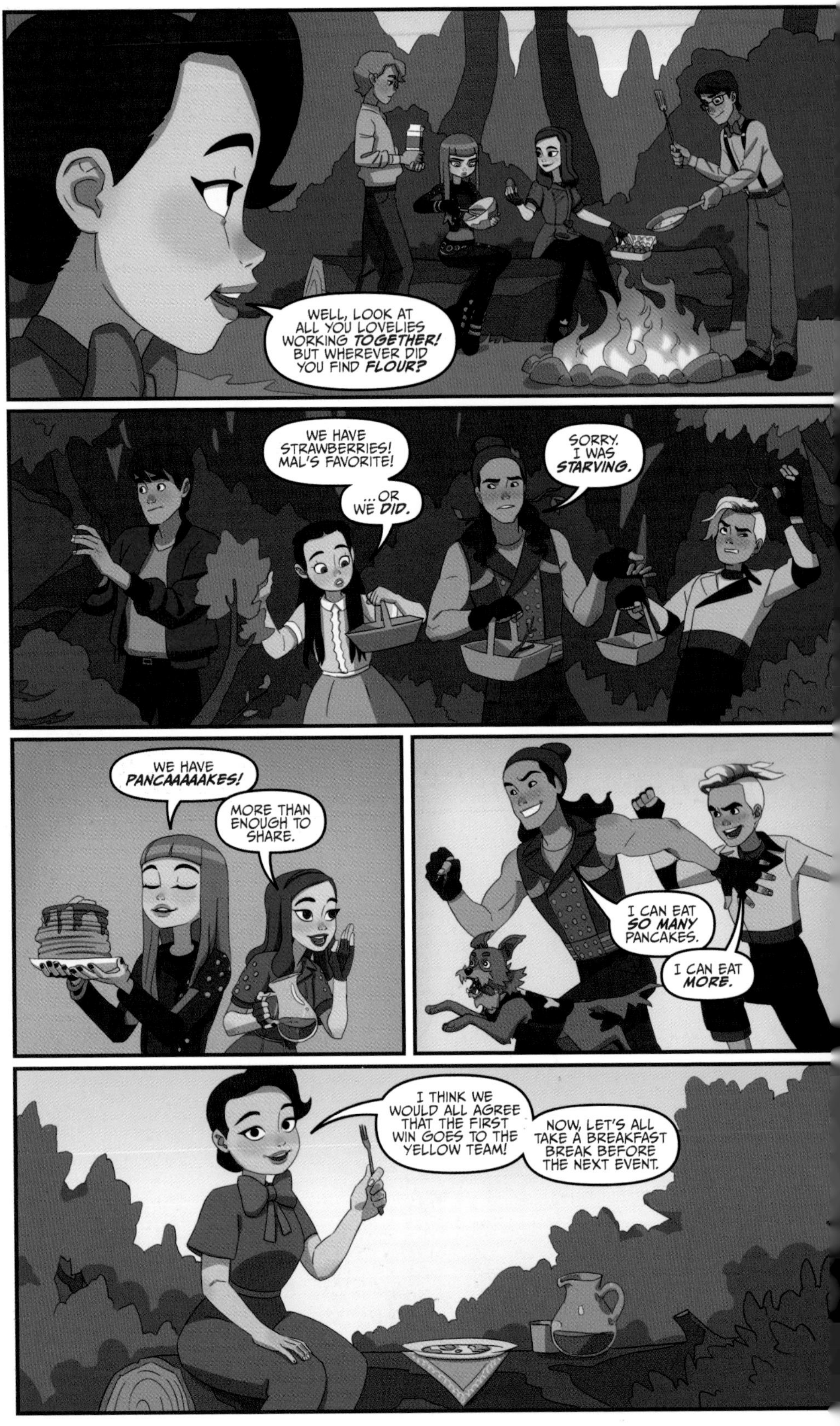
WELL, LOOK AT ALL YOU LOVELIES WORKING TOGETHER! BUT WHEREVER DID YOU FIND FLOUR?
WE HAVE STRAWBERRIES! MAL'S FAVORITE!
...OR WE DID.
SORRY. I WAS STARVING.
WE HAVE PANCAAAAAKES!
MORE THAN ENOUGH TO SHARE.
I CAN EAT SO MANY PANCAKES.
I CAN EAT MORE.
I THINK WE WOULD ALL AGREE THAT THE FIRST WIN GOES TO THE YELLOW TEAM!
NOW, LET'S ALL TAKE A BREAKFAST BREAK BEFORE THE NEXT EVENT.

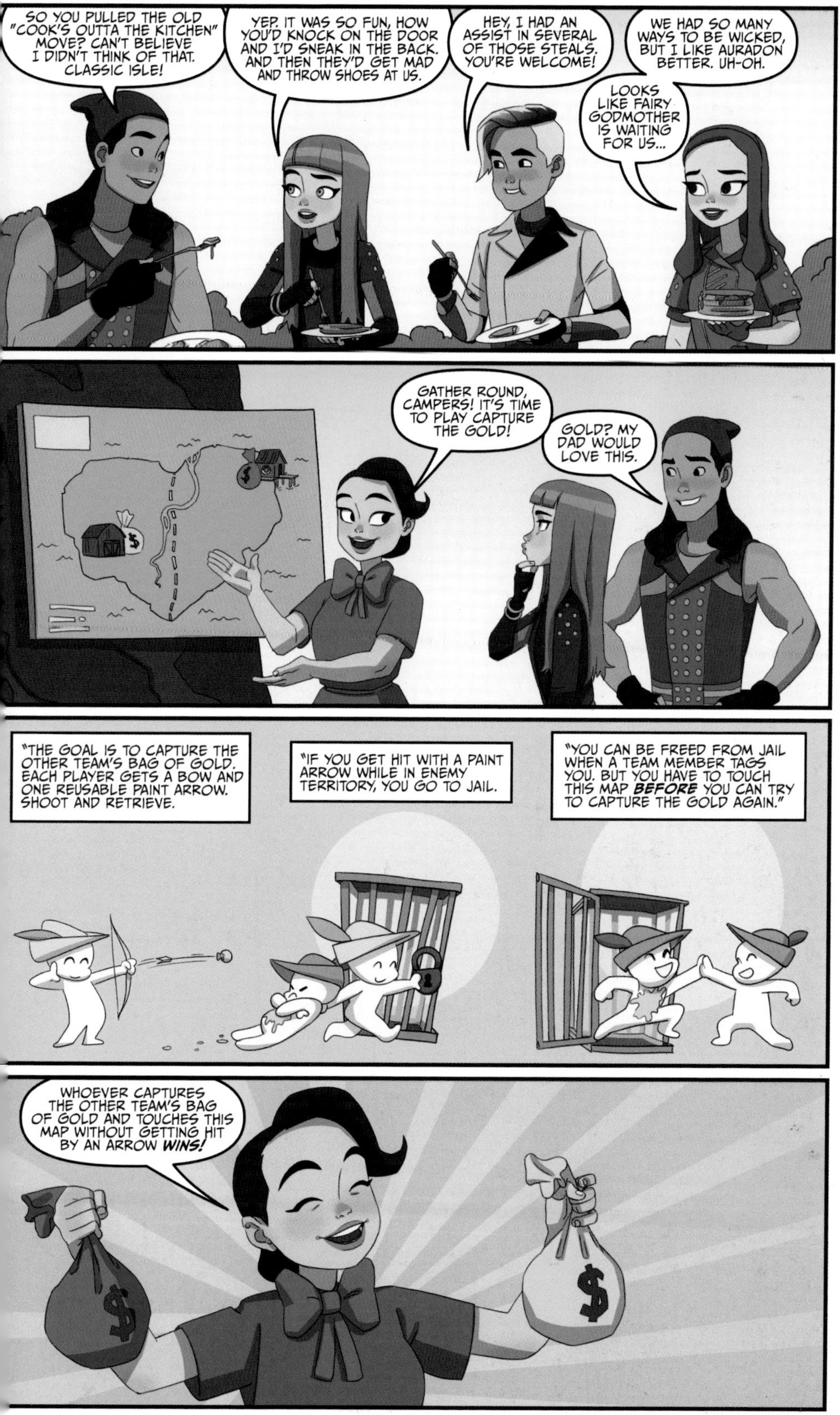
SO YOU PULLED THE OLD "COOK'S OUTTA THE KITCHEN" MOVE? CAN'T BELIEVE I DIDN'T THINK OF THAT. CLASSIC ISLE!
YEP. IT WAS SO FUN, HOW YOU'D KNOCK ON THE DOOR AND I'D SNEAK IN THE BACK. AND THEN THEY'D GET MAD AND THROW SHOES AT US.
HEY, I HAD AN ASSIST IN SEVERAL OF THOSE STEALS. YOU'RE WELCOME!
WE HAD SO MANY WAYS TO BE WICKED, BUT I LIKE AURADON BETTER. UH-OH.
LOOKS LIKE FAIRY GODMOTHER IS WAITING FOR US...
GATHER ROUND, CAMPERS! IT'S TIME TO PLAY CAPTURE THE GOLD!
GOLD? MY DAD WOULD LOVE THIS.
"THE GOAL IS TO CAPTURE THE OTHER TEAM'S BAG OF GOLD. EACH PLAYER GETS A BOW AND ONE REUSABLE PAINT ARROW. SHOOT AND RETRIEVE.
"IF YOU GET HIT WITH A PAINT ARROW WHILE IN ENEMY TERRITORY, YOU GO TO JAIL.
"YOU CAN BE FREED FROM JAIL WHEN A TEAM MEMBER TAGS YOU. BUT YOU HAVE TO TOUCH THIS MAP BEFORE YOU CAN TRY TO CAPTURE THE GOLD AGAIN."
WHOEVER CAPTURES THE OTHER TEAM'S BAG OF GOLD AND TOUCHES THIS MAP WITHOUT GETTING HIT BY AN ARROW WINS!

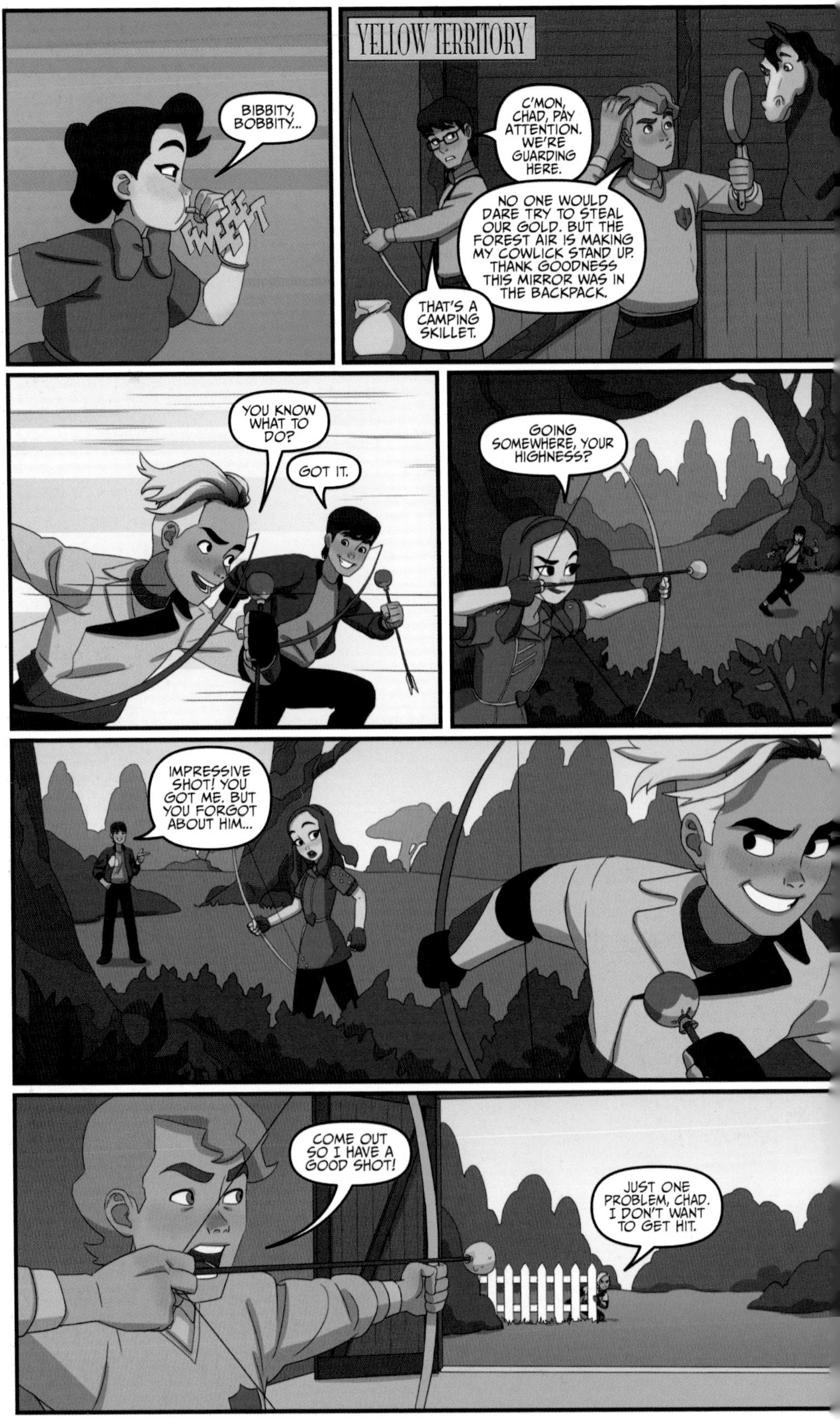
BIBBITY, BOBBITY...
TWEEEET
YELLOW TERRITORY
C'MON, CHAD, PAY ATTENTION. WE'RE GUARDING HERE.
NO ONE WOULD DARE TRY TO STEAL OUR GOLD. BUT THE FOREST AIR IS MAKING MY COWLICK STAND UP. THANK GOODNESS THIS MIRROR WAS IN THE BACKPACK.
THAT'S A CAMPING SKILLET.
YOU KNOW WHAT TO DO?
GOT IT.
GOING SOMEWHERE, YOUR HIGHNESS?
IMPRESSIVE SHOT! YOU GOT ME. BUT YOU FORGOT ABOUT HIM...
COME OUT SO I HAVE A GOOD SHOT!
JUST ONE PROBLEM, CHAD. I DON'T WANT TO GET HIT.

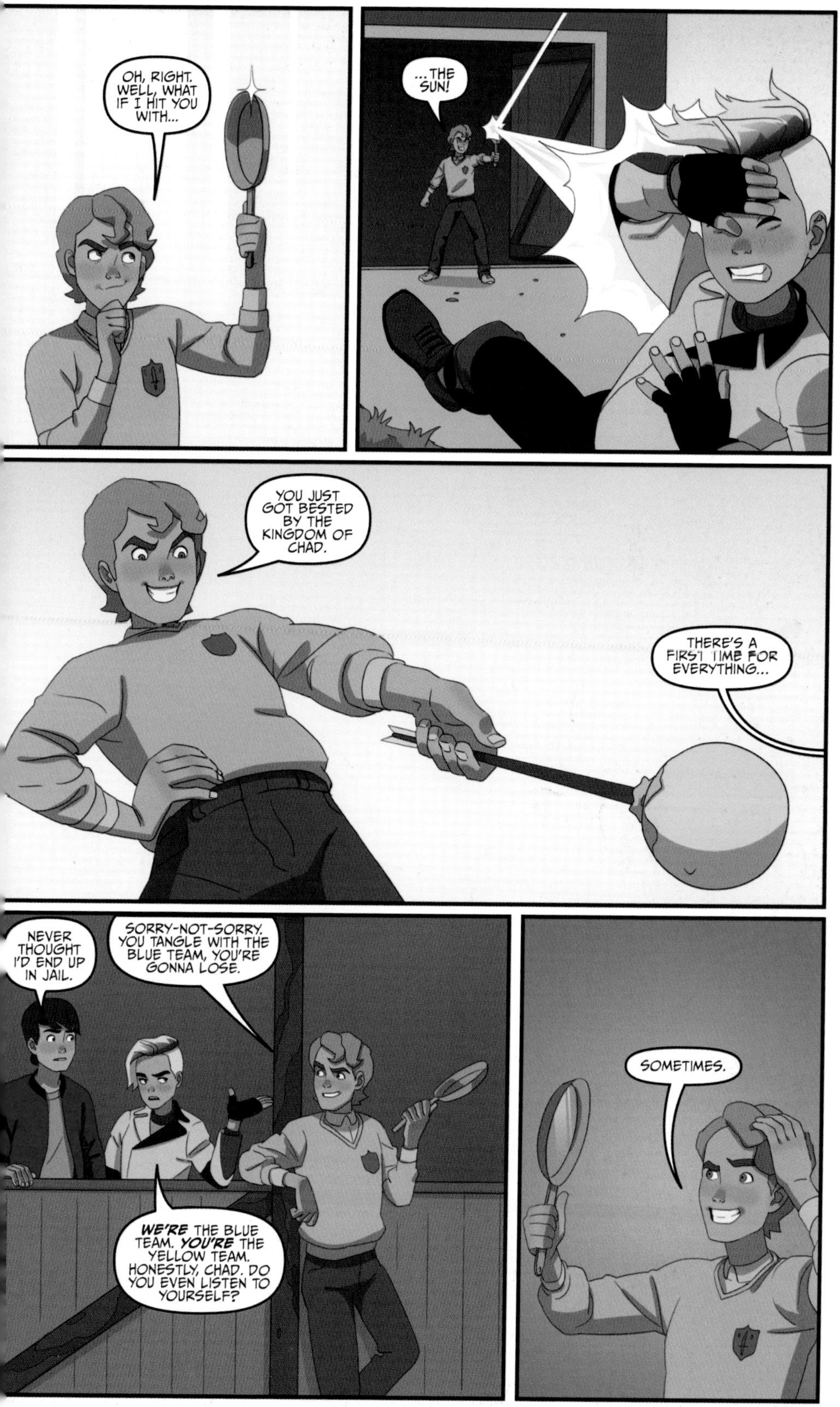
OH, RIGHT. WELL, WHAT IF I HIT YOU WITH...
...THE SUN!
YOU JUST GOT BESTED BY THE KINGDOM OF CHAD.
THERE'S A FIRST TIME FOR EVERYTHING...
NEVER THOUGHT I'D END UP IN JAIL.
SORRY-NOT-SORRY. YOU TANGLE WITH THE BLUE TEAM, YOU'RE GONNA LOSE.
WE'RE THE BLUE TEAM. *YOU'RE* THE YELLOW TEAM. HONESTLY, CHAD. DO YOU EVEN LISTEN TO YOURSELF?
SOMETIMES.

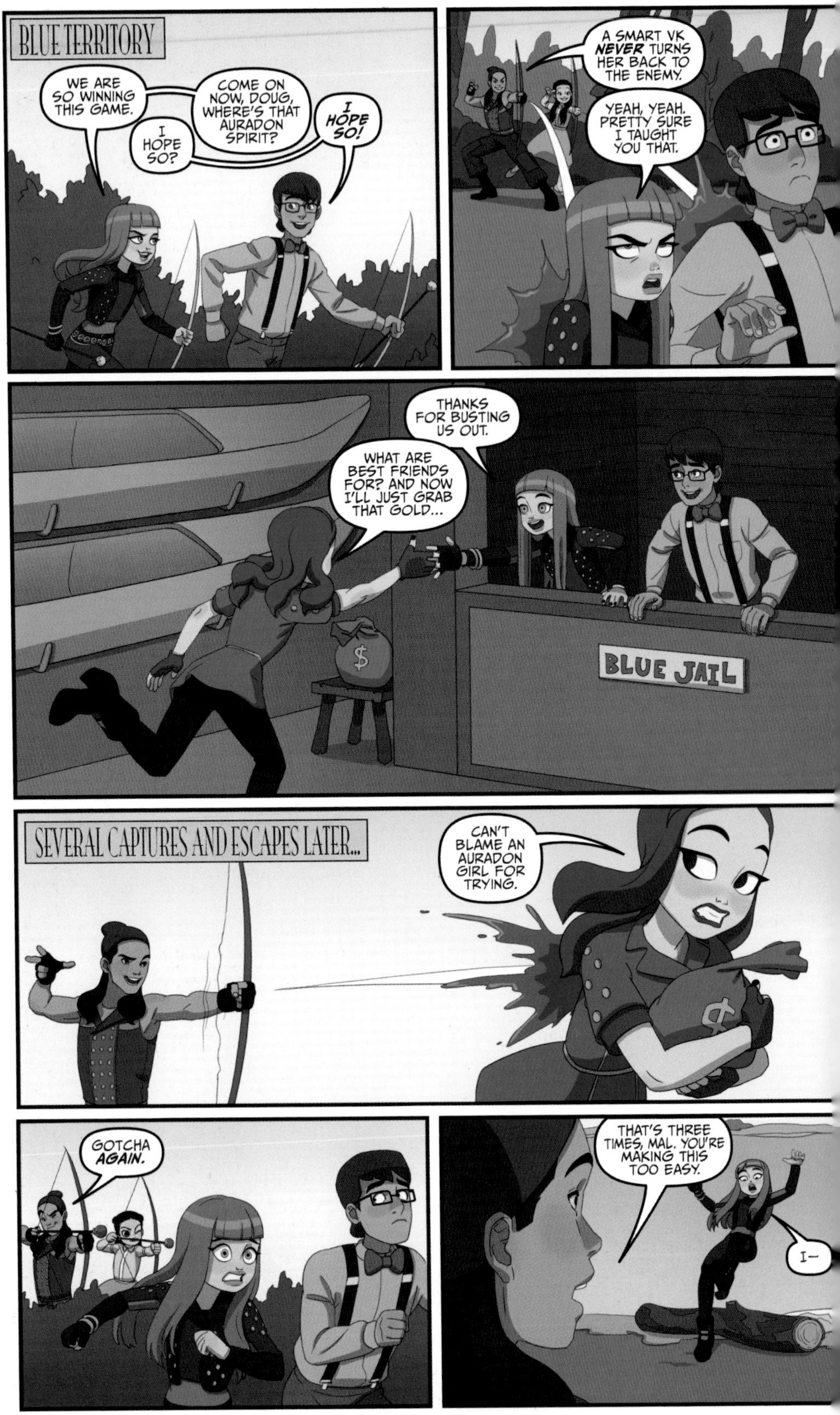

BLUE TERRITORY
WE ARE SO WINNING THIS GAME.
COME ON NOW, DOUG, WHERE'S THAT AURADON SPIRIT?
I HOPE SO?
I HOPE SO!
A SMART VK NEVER TURNS HER BACK TO THE ENEMY.
YEAH, YEAH. PRETTY SURE I TAUGHT YOU THAT.
THANKS FOR BUSTING US OUT.
WHAT ARE BEST FRIENDS FOR? AND NOW I'LL JUST GRAB THAT GOLD...
BLUE JAIL
SEVERAL CAPTURES AND ESCAPES LATER...
CAN'T BLAME AN AURADON GIRL FOR TRYING.
GOTCHA AGAIN.
THAT'S THREE TIMES, MAL. YOU'RE MAKING THIS TOO EASY.
I—

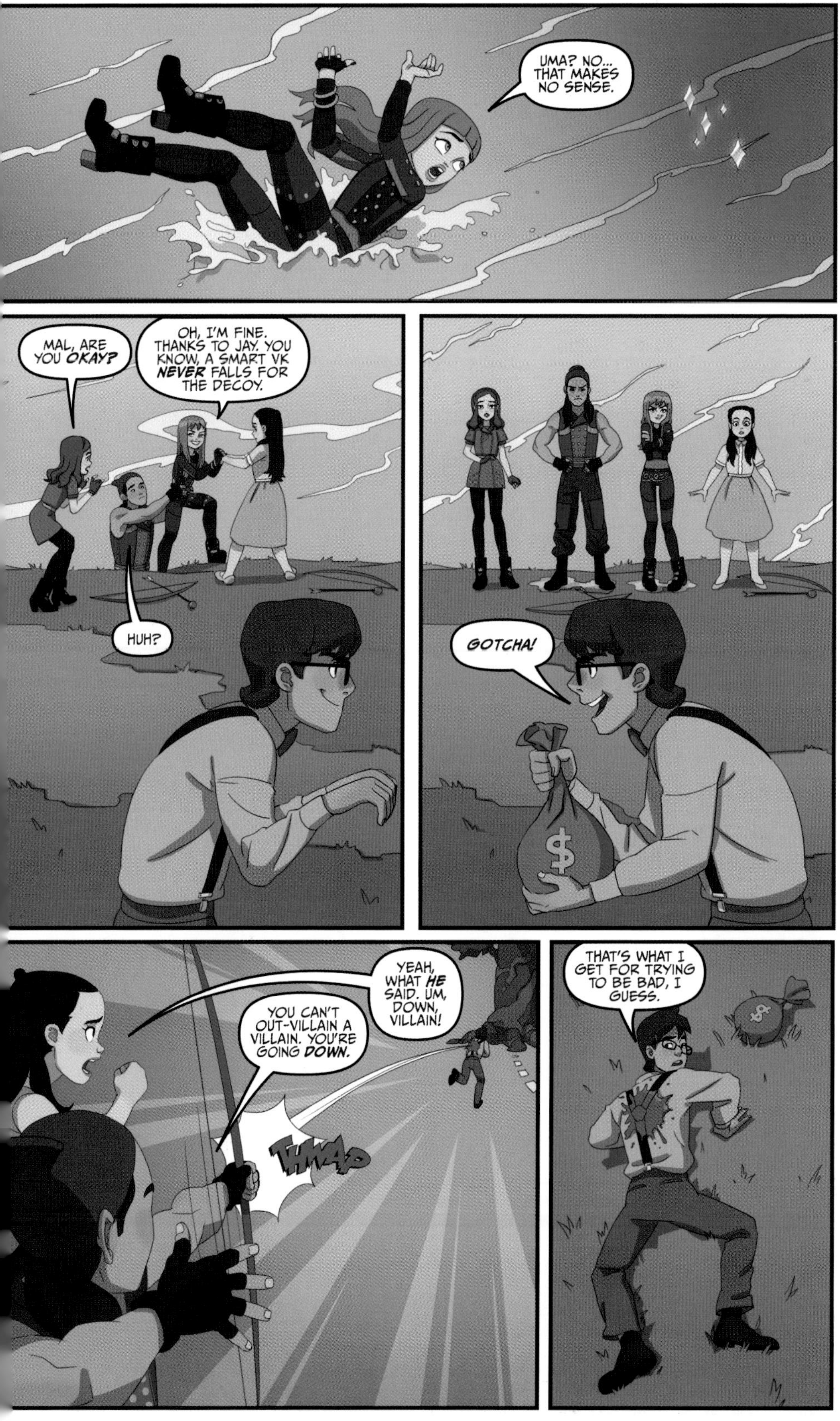
UMA? NO... THAT MAKES NO SENSE.
MAL, ARE YOU **OKAY?**
OH, I'M FINE. THANKS TO JAY. YOU KNOW, A SMART VK **NEVER** FALLS FOR THE DECOY.
HUH?
GOTCHA!
YOU CAN'T OUT-VILLAIN A VILLAIN. YOU'RE GOING **DOWN.**
YEAH, WHAT **HE** SAID. UM, DOWN, VILLAIN!
THWAP
THAT'S WHAT I GET FOR TRYING TO BE BAD, I GUESS.

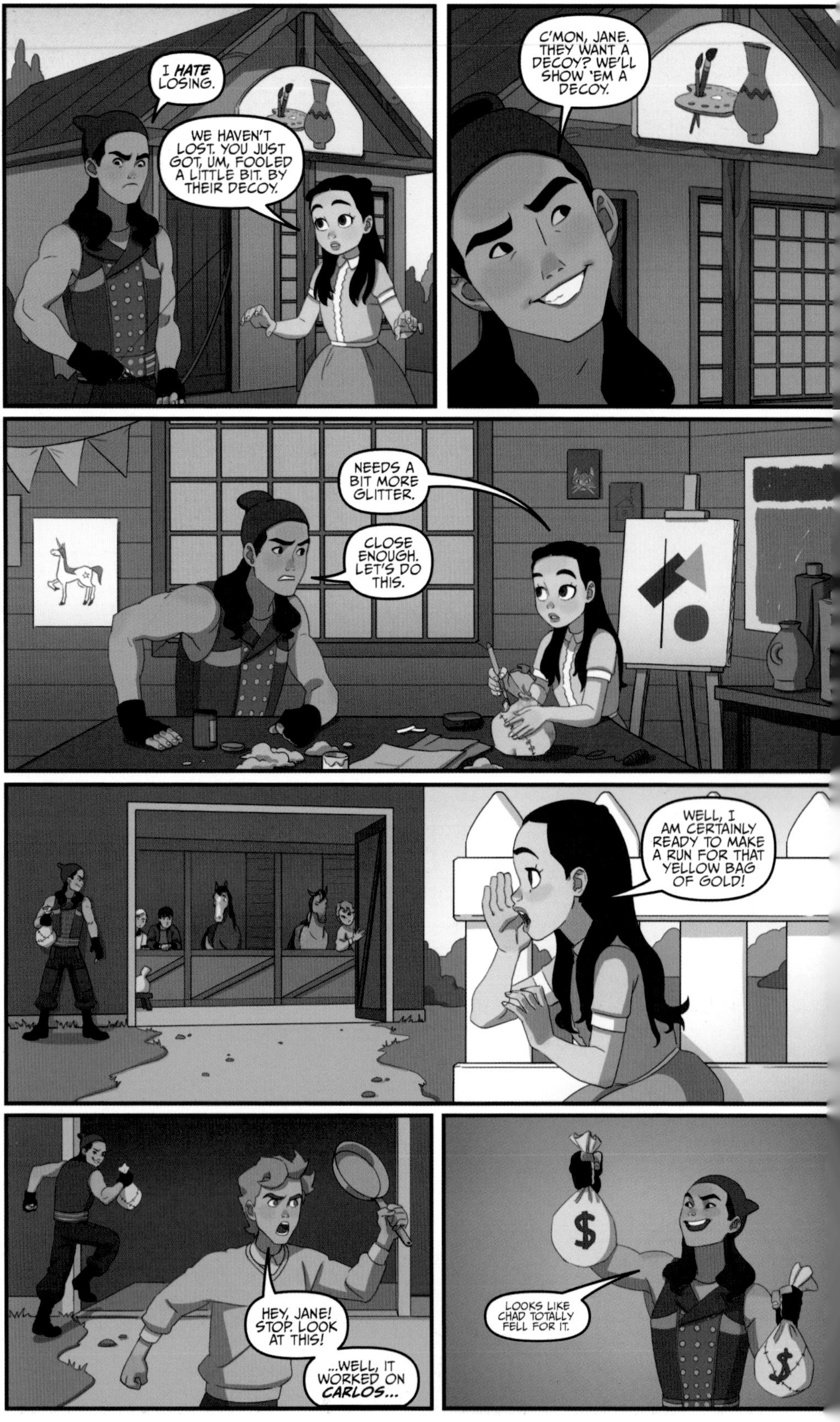
I HATE LOSING.
WE HAVEN'T LOST. YOU JUST GOT, UM, FOOLED A LITTLE BIT. BY THEIR DECOY.
C'MON, JANE. THEY WANT A DECOY? WE'LL SHOW 'EM A DECOY.
NEEDS A BIT MORE GLITTER.
CLOSE ENOUGH. LET'S DO THIS.
WELL, I AM CERTAINLY READY TO MAKE A RUN FOR THAT YELLOW BAG OF GOLD!
HEY, JANE! STOP. LOOK AT THIS!
...WELL, IT WORKED ON CARLOS...
LOOKS LIKE CHAD TOTALLY FELL FOR IT.

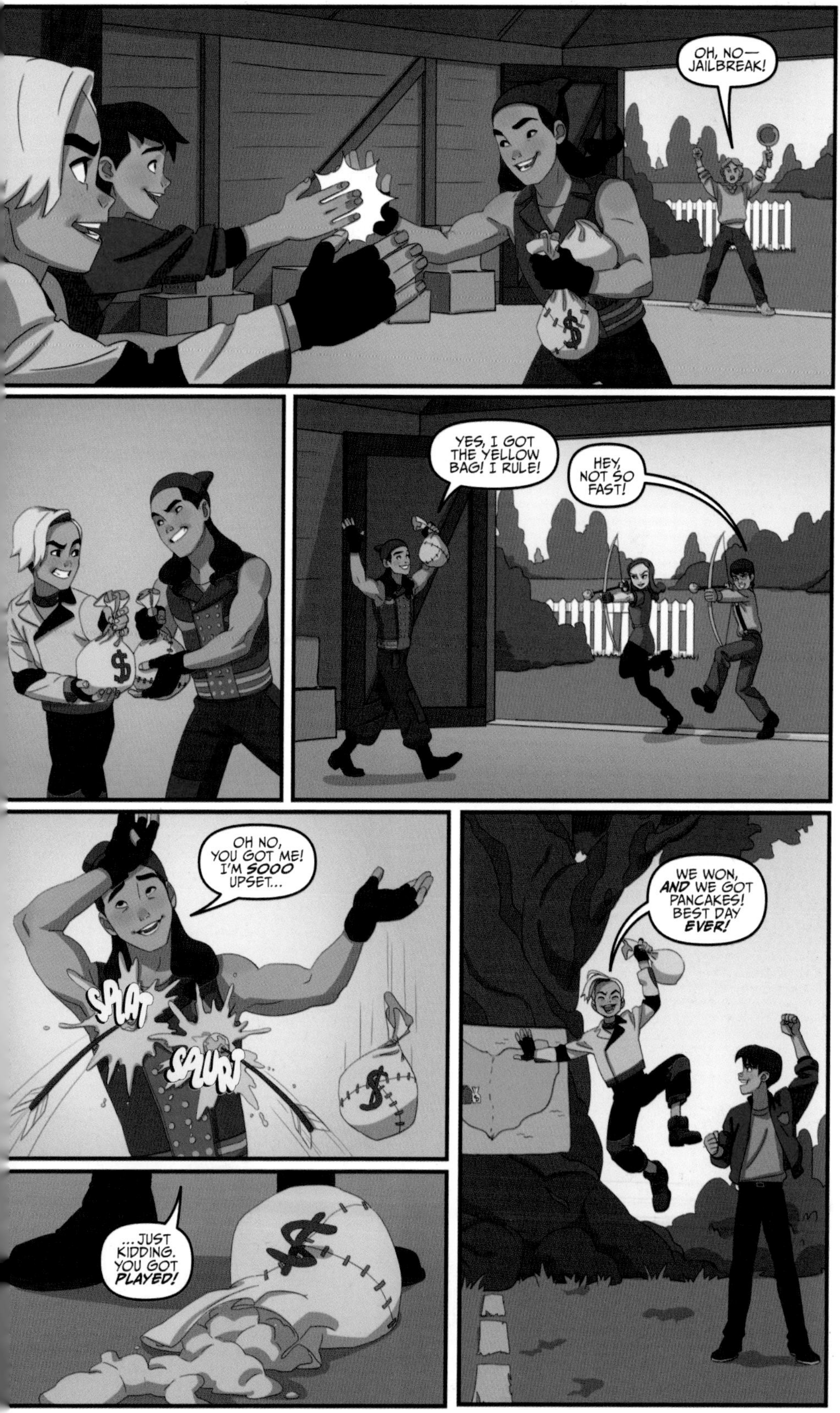
OH, NO—
JAILBREAK!
YES, I GOT THE YELLOW BAG! I RULE!
HEY, NOT SO FAST!
OH NO, YOU GOT ME! I'M *SOOO* UPSET...
SPLAT
SPLURT
...JUST KIDDING. YOU GOT ***PLAYED!***
WE WON, ***AND*** WE GOT PANCAKES! BEST DAY ***EVER!***

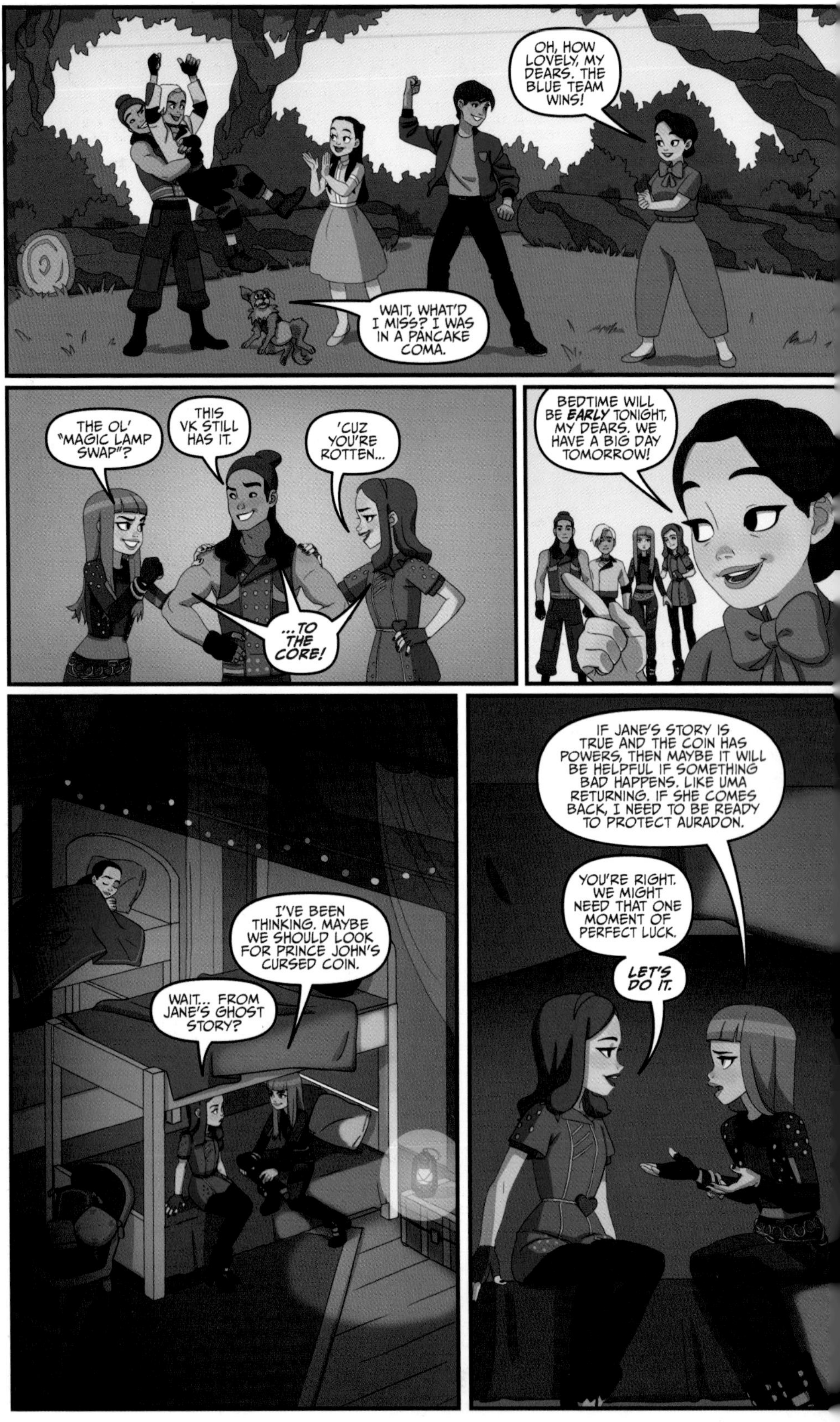
OH, HOW LOVELY, MY DEARS. THE BLUE TEAM WINS!
WAIT, WHAT'D I MISS? I WAS IN A PANCAKE COMA.
THE OL' "MAGIC LAMP SWAP"?
THIS VK STILL HAS IT.
'CUZ YOU'RE ROTTEN...
...TO THE CORE!
BEDTIME WILL BE EARLY TONIGHT, MY DEARS. WE HAVE A BIG DAY TOMORROW!
I'VE BEEN THINKING. MAYBE WE SHOULD LOOK FOR PRINCE JOHN'S CURSED COIN.
WAIT... FROM JANE'S GHOST STORY?
IF JANE'S STORY IS TRUE AND THE COIN HAS POWERS, THEN MAYBE IT WILL BE HELPFUL IF SOMETHING BAD HAPPENS. LIKE UMA RETURNING. IF SHE COMES BACK, I NEED TO BE READY TO PROTECT AURADON.
YOU'RE RIGHT. WE MIGHT NEED THAT ONE MOMENT OF PERFECT LUCK.
LET'S DO IT.

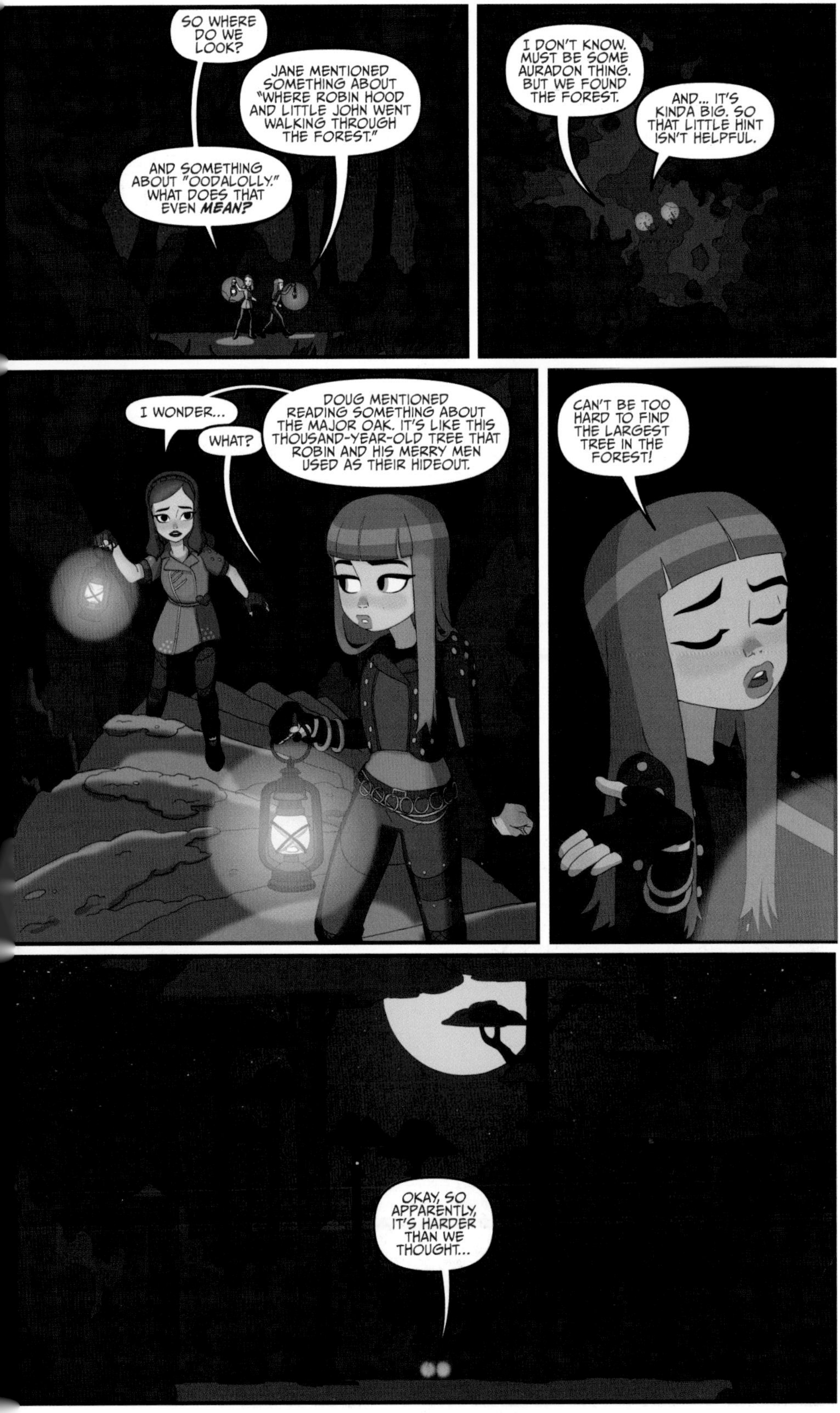
SO WHERE DO WE LOOK?
JANE MENTIONED SOMETHING ABOUT "WHERE ROBIN HOOD AND LITTLE JOHN WENT WALKING THROUGH THE FOREST."
AND SOMETHING ABOUT "OODALOLLY." WHAT DOES THAT EVEN ***MEAN?***
I DON'T KNOW. MUST BE SOME AURADON THING. BUT WE FOUND THE FOREST.
AND... IT'S KINDA BIG. SO THAT LITTLE HINT ISN'T HELPFUL.
I WONDER...
WHAT?
DOUG MENTIONED READING SOMETHING ABOUT THE MAJOR OAK. IT'S LIKE THIS THOUSAND-YEAR-OLD TREE THAT ROBIN AND HIS MERRY MEN USED AS THEIR HIDEOUT.
CAN'T BE TOO HARD TO FIND THE LARGEST TREE IN THE FOREST!
OKAY, SO APPARENTLY, IT'S HARDER THAN WE THOUGHT...

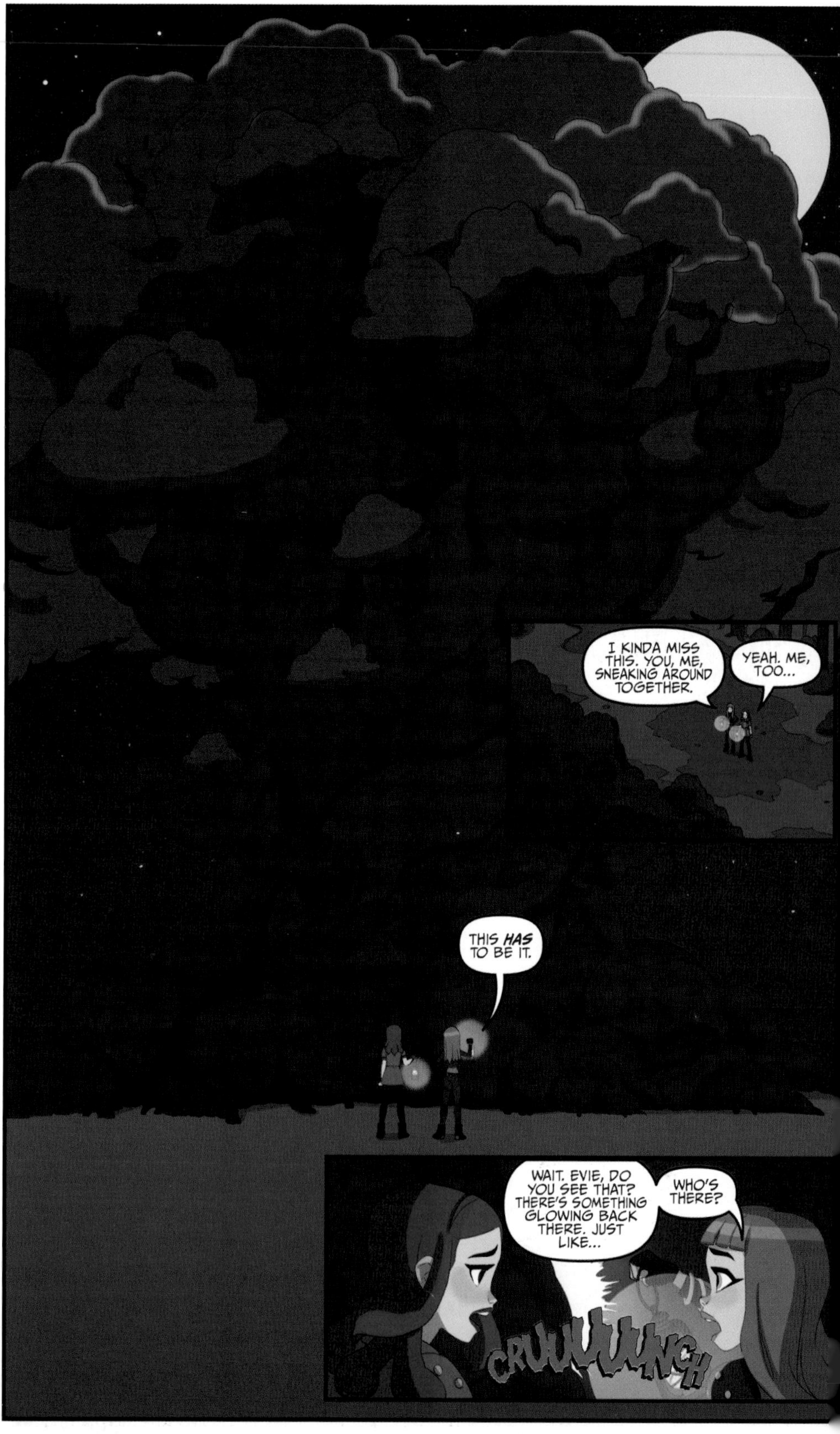
I KINDA MISS THIS. YOU, ME, SNEAKING AROUND TOGETHER.
YEAH. ME, TOO...
THIS **HAS** TO BE IT.
WAIT. EVIE, DO YOU SEE THAT? THERE'S SOMETHING GLOWING BACK THERE. JUST LIKE...
WHO'S THERE?
CRUUUUUNCH

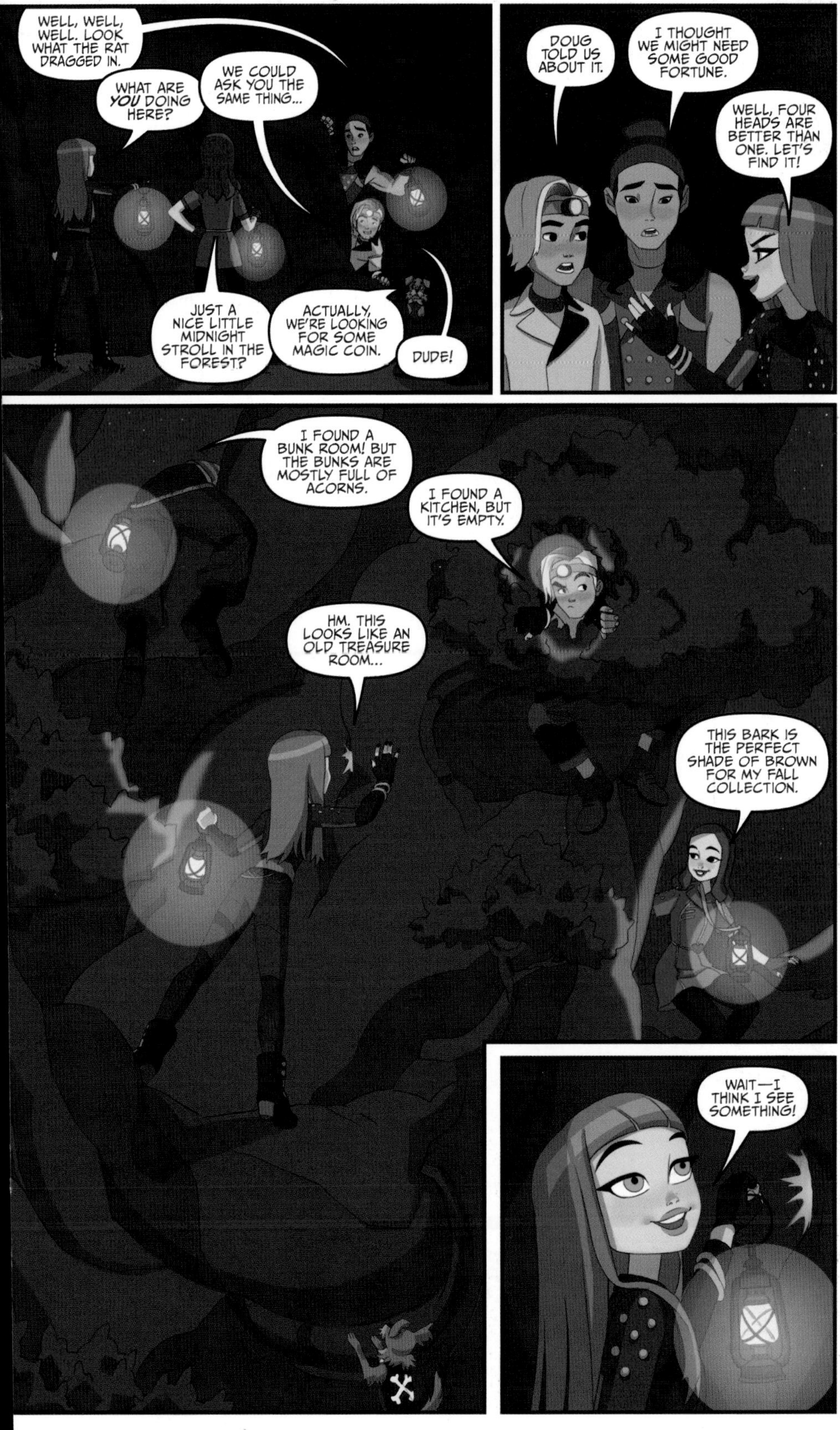
WELL, WELL, WELL. LOOK WHAT THE RAT DRAGGED IN.
WHAT ARE *YOU* DOING HERE?
WE COULD ASK YOU THE SAME THING...
JUST A NICE LITTLE MIDNIGHT STROLL IN THE FOREST?
ACTUALLY, WE'RE LOOKING FOR SOME MAGIC COIN.
DUDE!
DOUG TOLD US ABOUT IT.
I THOUGHT WE MIGHT NEED SOME GOOD FORTUNE.
WELL, FOUR HEADS ARE BETTER THAN ONE. LET'S FIND IT!
I FOUND A BUNK ROOM! BUT THE BUNKS ARE MOSTLY FULL OF ACORNS.
I FOUND A KITCHEN, BUT IT'S EMPTY.
HM. THIS LOOKS LIKE AN OLD TREASURE ROOM...
THIS BARK IS THE PERFECT SHADE OF BROWN FOR MY FALL COLLECTION.
WAIT—I THINK I SEE SOMETHING!

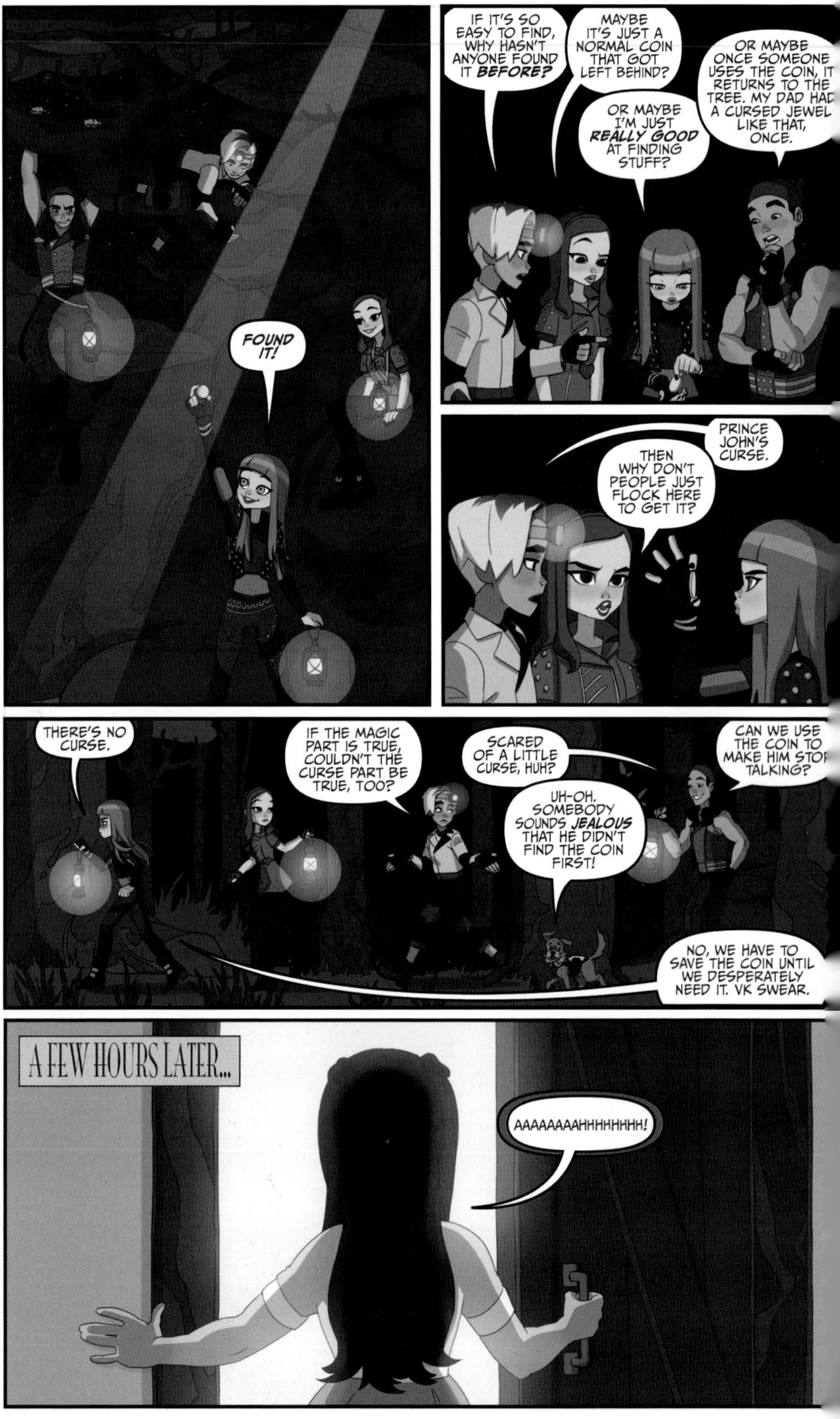
FOUND IT!
IF IT'S SO EASY TO FIND, WHY HASN'T ANYONE FOUND IT BEFORE?
MAYBE IT'S JUST A NORMAL COIN THAT GOT LEFT BEHIND?
OR MAYBE I'M JUST REALLY GOOD AT FINDING STUFF?
OR MAYBE ONCE SOMEONE USES THE COIN, IT RETURNS TO THE TREE. MY DAD HAD A CURSED JEWEL LIKE THAT, ONCE.
THEN WHY DON'T PEOPLE JUST FLOCK HERE TO GET IT?
PRINCE JOHN'S CURSE.
THERE'S NO CURSE.
IF THE MAGIC PART IS TRUE, COULDN'T THE CURSE PART BE TRUE, TOO?
SCARED OF A LITTLE CURSE, HUH?
UH-OH. SOMEBODY SOUNDS JEALOUS THAT HE DIDN'T FIND THE COIN FIRST!
CAN WE USE THE COIN TO MAKE HIM STOP TALKING?
NO, WE HAVE TO SAVE THE COIN UNTIL WE DESPERATELY NEED IT. VK SWEAR.
A FEW HOURS LATER...
AAAAAAAAHHHHHHHH!

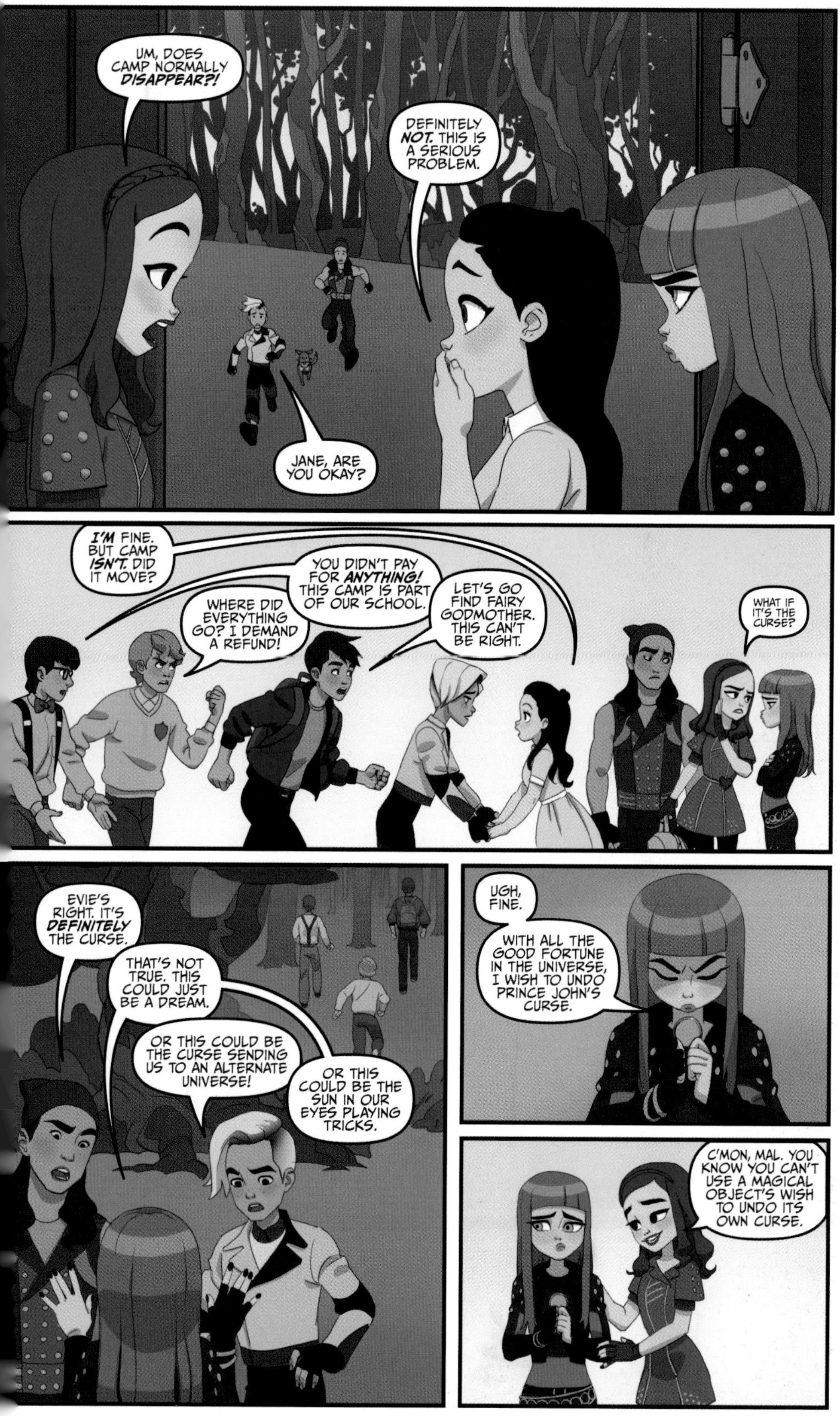

UM, DOES CAMP NORMALLY DISAPPEAR?!
DEFINITELY NOT. THIS IS A SERIOUS PROBLEM.
JANE, ARE YOU OKAY?
I'M FINE. BUT CAMP ISN'T. DID IT MOVE?
WHERE DID EVERYTHING GO? I DEMAND A REFUND!
YOU DIDN'T PAY FOR ANYTHING! THIS CAMP IS PART OF OUR SCHOOL.
LET'S GO FIND FAIRY GODMOTHER. THIS CAN'T BE RIGHT.
WHAT IF IT'S THE CURSE?
EVIE'S RIGHT. IT'S DEFINITELY THE CURSE.
THAT'S NOT TRUE. THIS COULD JUST BE A DREAM.
OR THIS COULD BE THE CURSE SENDING US TO AN ALTERNATE UNIVERSE!
OR THIS COULD BE THE SUN IN OUR EYES PLAYING TRICKS.
UGH, FINE.
WITH ALL THE GOOD FORTUNE IN THE UNIVERSE, I WISH TO UNDO PRINCE JOHN'S CURSE.
C'MON, MAL. YOU KNOW YOU CAN'T USE A MAGICAL OBJECT'S WISH TO UNDO ITS OWN CURSE.

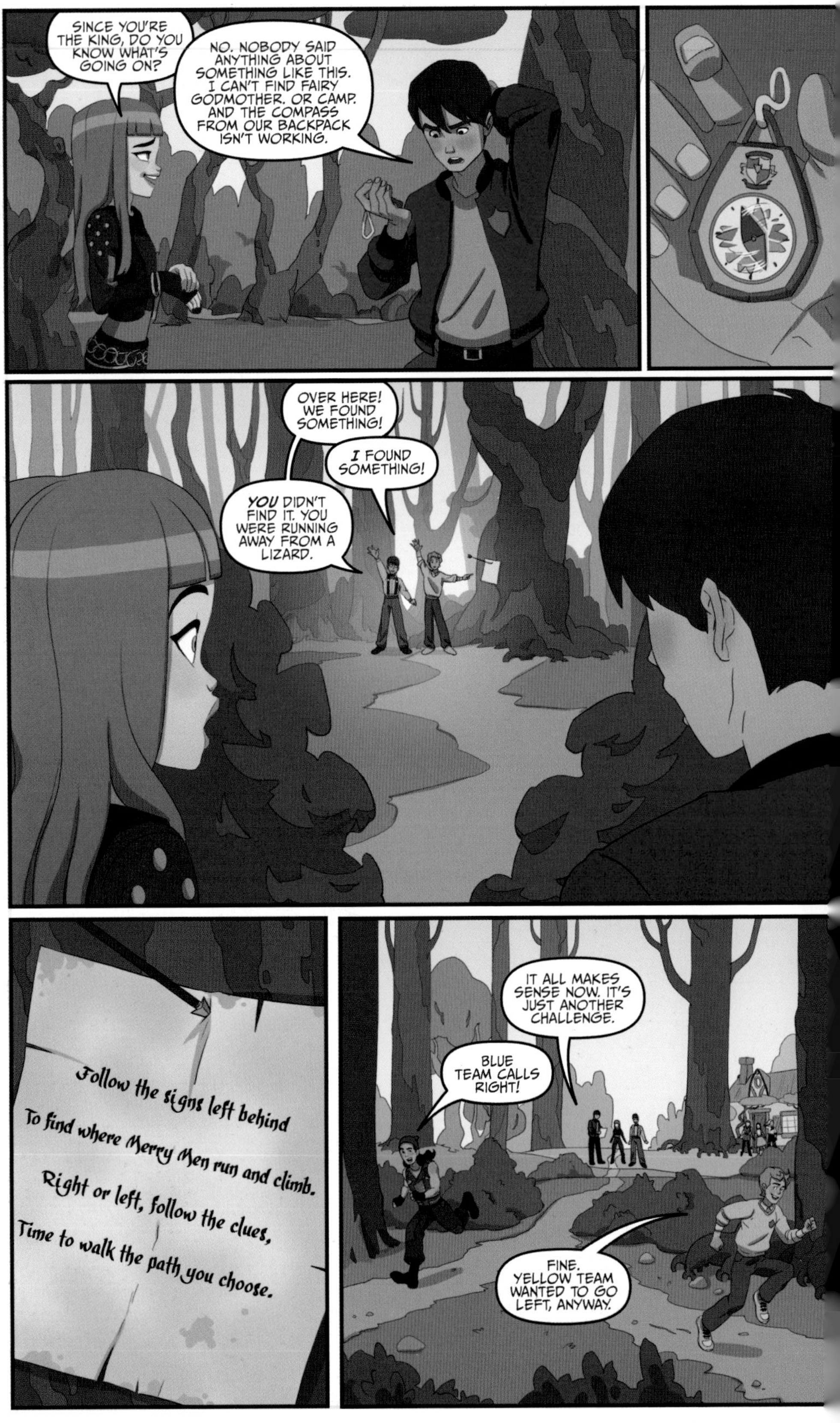
SINCE YOU'RE THE KING, DO YOU KNOW WHAT'S GOING ON?
NO. NOBODY SAID ANYTHING ABOUT SOMETHING LIKE THIS. I CAN'T FIND FAIRY GODMOTHER. OR CAMP. AND THE COMPASS FROM OUR BACKPACK ISN'T WORKING.
OVER HERE! WE FOUND SOMETHING!
I FOUND SOMETHING!
YOU DIDN'T FIND IT. YOU WERE RUNNING AWAY FROM A LIZARD.
Follow the signs left behind
To find where Merry Men run and climb.
Right or left, follow the clues,
Time to walk the path you choose.
IT ALL MAKES SENSE NOW. IT'S JUST ANOTHER CHALLENGE.
BLUE TEAM CALLS RIGHT!
FINE. YELLOW TEAM WANTED TO GO LEFT, ANYWAY.

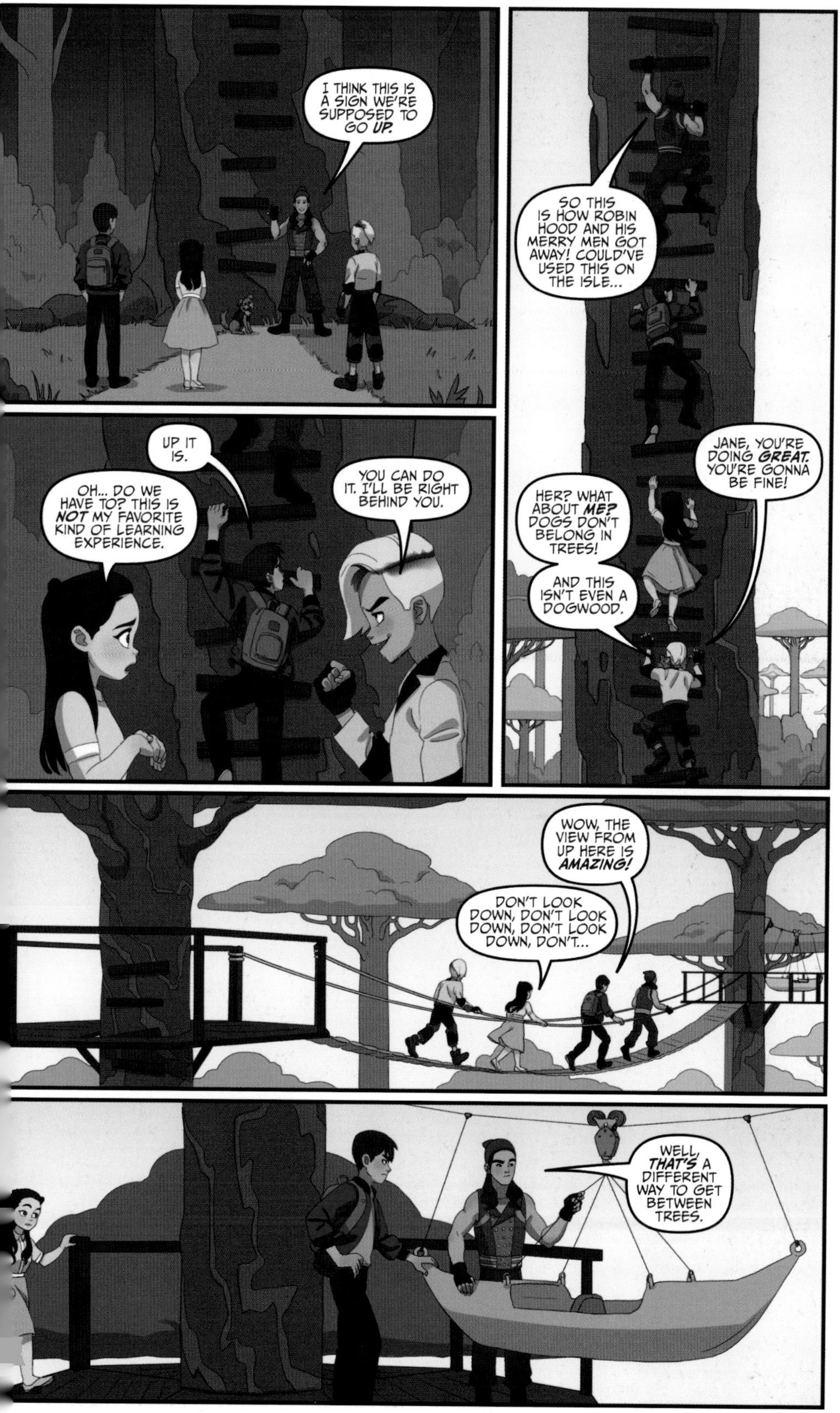
I THINK THIS IS A SIGN WE'RE SUPPOSED TO GO *UP.*
UP IT IS.
OH... DO WE HAVE TO? THIS IS *NOT* MY FAVORITE KIND OF LEARNING EXPERIENCE.
YOU CAN DO IT. I'LL BE RIGHT BEHIND YOU.
SO THIS IS HOW ROBIN HOOD AND HIS MERRY MEN GOT AWAY! COULD'VE USED THIS ON THE ISLE...
JANE, YOU'RE DOING *GREAT.* YOU'RE GONNA BE FINE!
HER? WHAT ABOUT *ME?* DOGS DON'T BELONG IN TREES!
AND THIS ISN'T EVEN A DOGWOOD.
WOW, THE VIEW FROM UP HERE IS *AMAZING!*
DON'T LOOK DOWN, DON'T LOOK DOWN, DON'T LOOK DOWN, DON'T...
WELL, *THAT'S* A DIFFERENT WAY TO GET BETWEEN TREES.

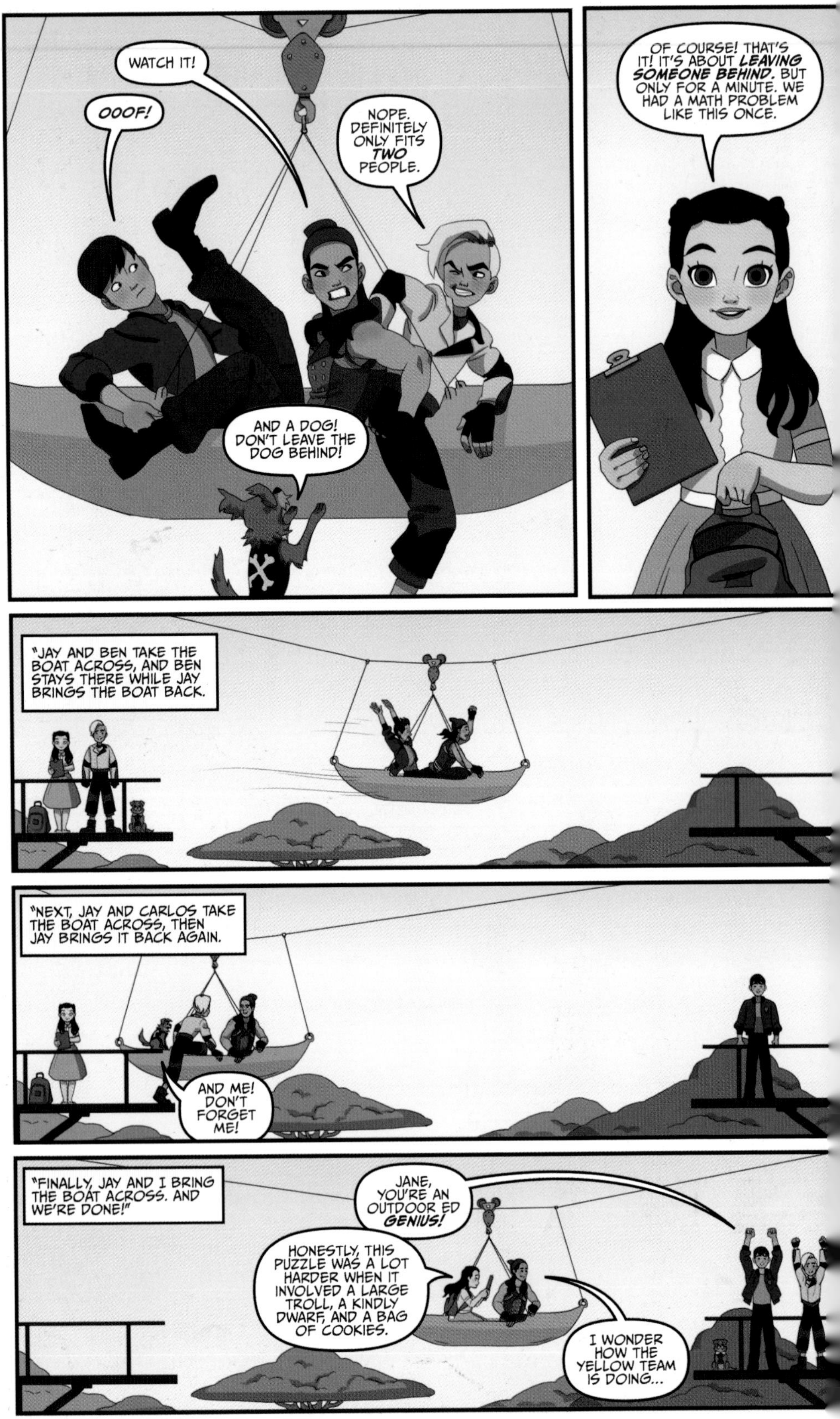
WATCH IT!
OOOF!
NOPE. DEFINITELY ONLY FITS TWO PEOPLE.
AND A DOG! DON'T LEAVE THE DOG BEHIND!
OF COURSE! THAT'S IT! IT'S ABOUT LEAVING SOMEONE BEHIND. BUT ONLY FOR A MINUTE. WE HAD A MATH PROBLEM LIKE THIS ONCE.
"JAY AND BEN TAKE THE BOAT ACROSS, AND BEN STAYS THERE WHILE JAY BRINGS THE BOAT BACK.
"NEXT, JAY AND CARLOS TAKE THE BOAT ACROSS, THEN JAY BRINGS IT BACK AGAIN.
AND ME! DON'T FORGET ME!
"FINALLY, JAY AND I BRING THE BOAT ACROSS. AND WE'RE DONE!"
JANE, YOU'RE AN OUTDOOR ED GENIUS!
HONESTLY, THIS PUZZLE WAS A LOT HARDER WHEN IT INVOLVED A LARGE TROLL, A KINDLY DWARF, AND A BAG OF COOKIES.
I WONDER HOW THE YELLOW TEAM IS DOING...

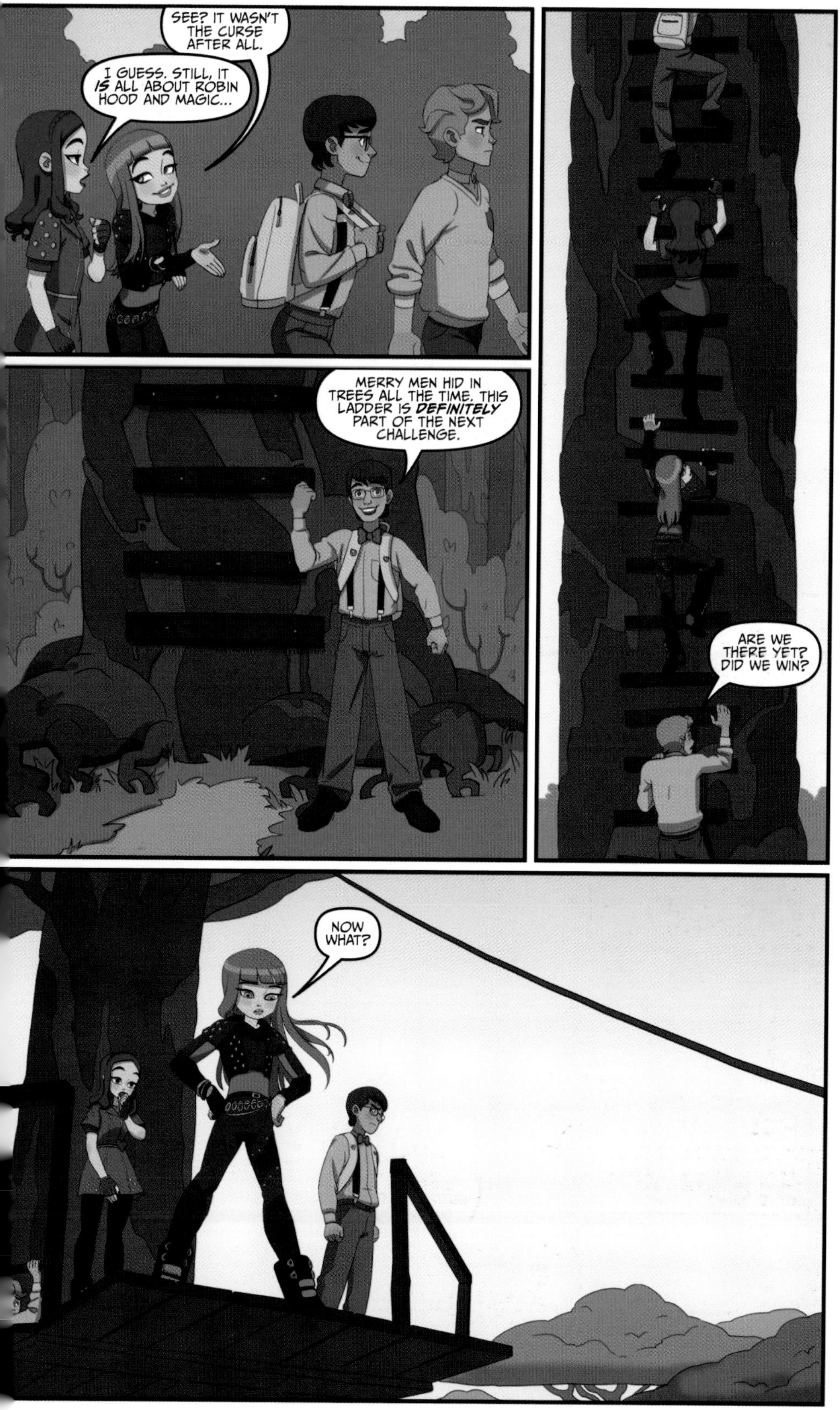
SEE? IT WASN'T THE CURSE AFTER ALL.
I GUESS. STILL, IT *IS* ALL ABOUT ROBIN HOOD AND MAGIC...
MERRY MEN HID IN TREES ALL THE TIME. THIS LADDER IS ***DEFINITELY*** PART OF THE NEXT CHALLENGE.
ARE WE THERE YET? DID WE WIN?
NOW WHAT?

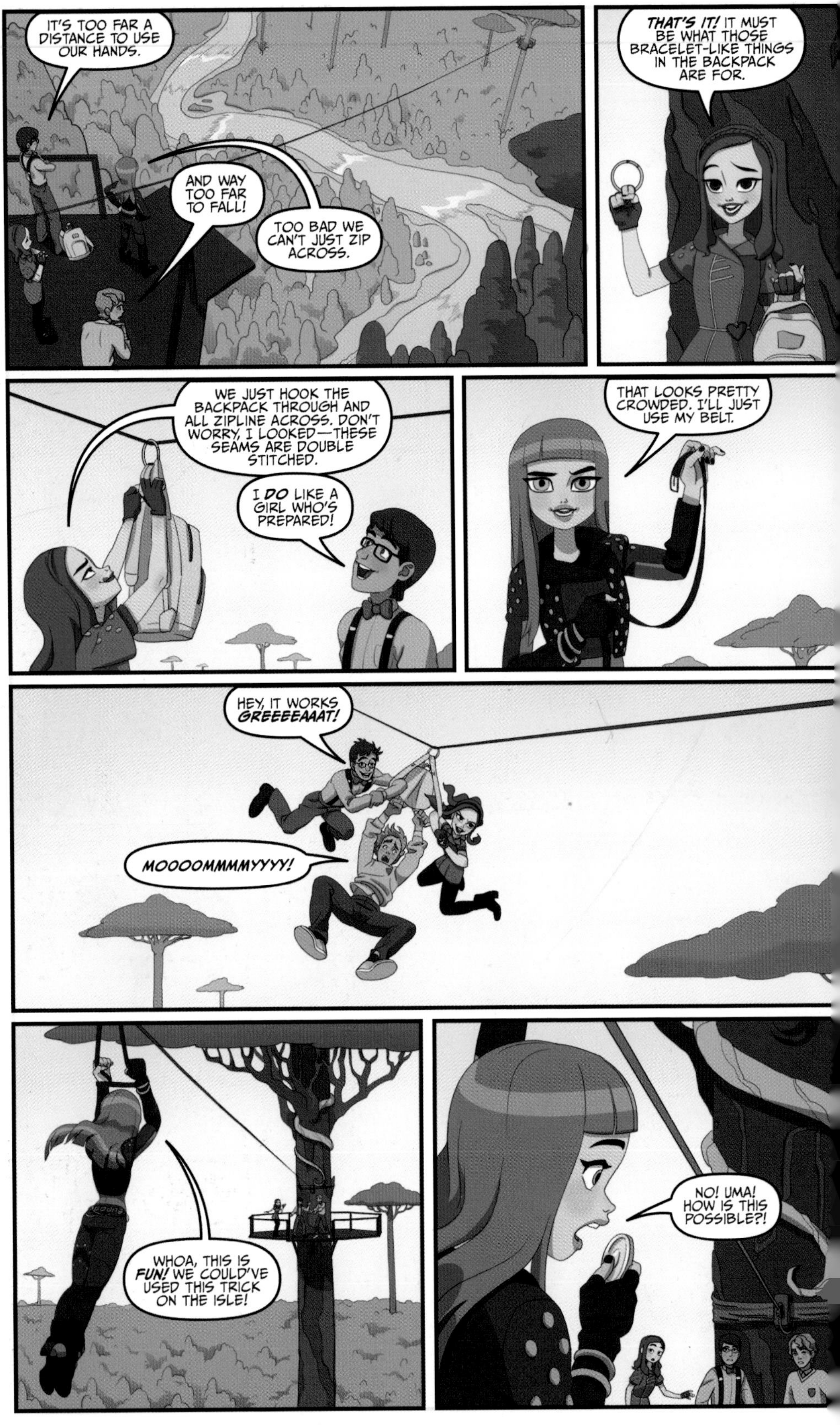
IT'S TOO FAR A DISTANCE TO USE OUR HANDS.
AND WAY TOO FAR TO FALL!
TOO BAD WE CAN'T JUST ZIP ACROSS.
THAT'S IT! IT MUST BE WHAT THOSE BRACELET-LIKE THINGS IN THE BACKPACK ARE FOR.
WE JUST HOOK THE BACKPACK THROUGH AND ALL ZIPLINE ACROSS. DON'T WORRY, I LOOKED—THESE SEAMS ARE DOUBLE STITCHED.
I DO LIKE A GIRL WHO'S PREPARED!
THAT LOOKS PRETTY CROWDED. I'LL JUST USE MY BELT.
HEY, IT WORKS GREEEEAAAT!
MOOOOMMMMYYYY!
WHOA, THIS IS FUN! WE COULD'VE USED THIS TRICK ON THE ISLE!
NO! UMA! HOW IS THIS POSSIBLE?!

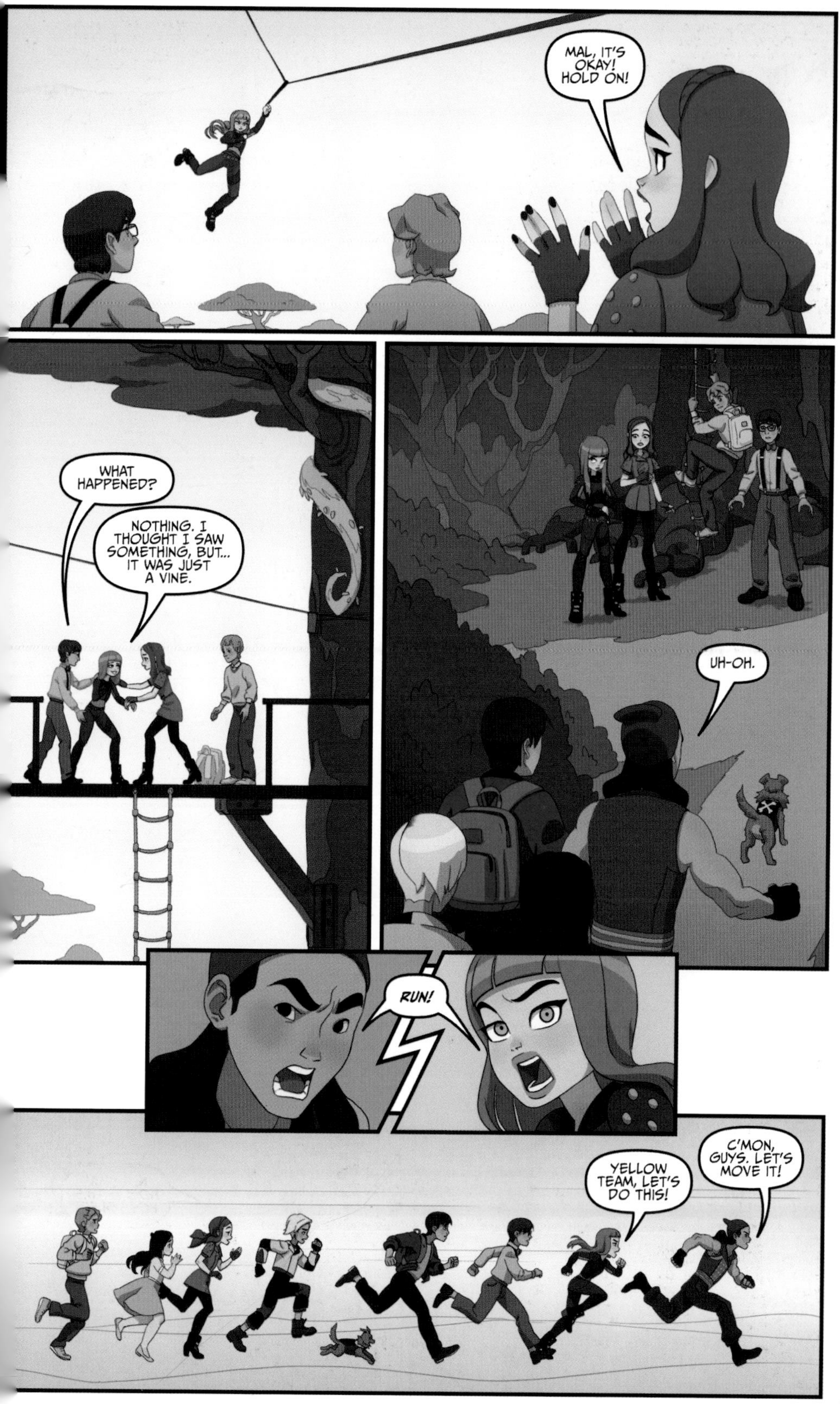
MAL, IT'S OKAY! HOLD ON!
WHAT HAPPENED?
NOTHING. I THOUGHT I SAW SOMETHING, BUT... IT WAS JUST A VINE.
UH-OH.
RUN!
C'MON, GUYS. LET'S MOVE IT!
YELLOW TEAM, LET'S DO THIS!

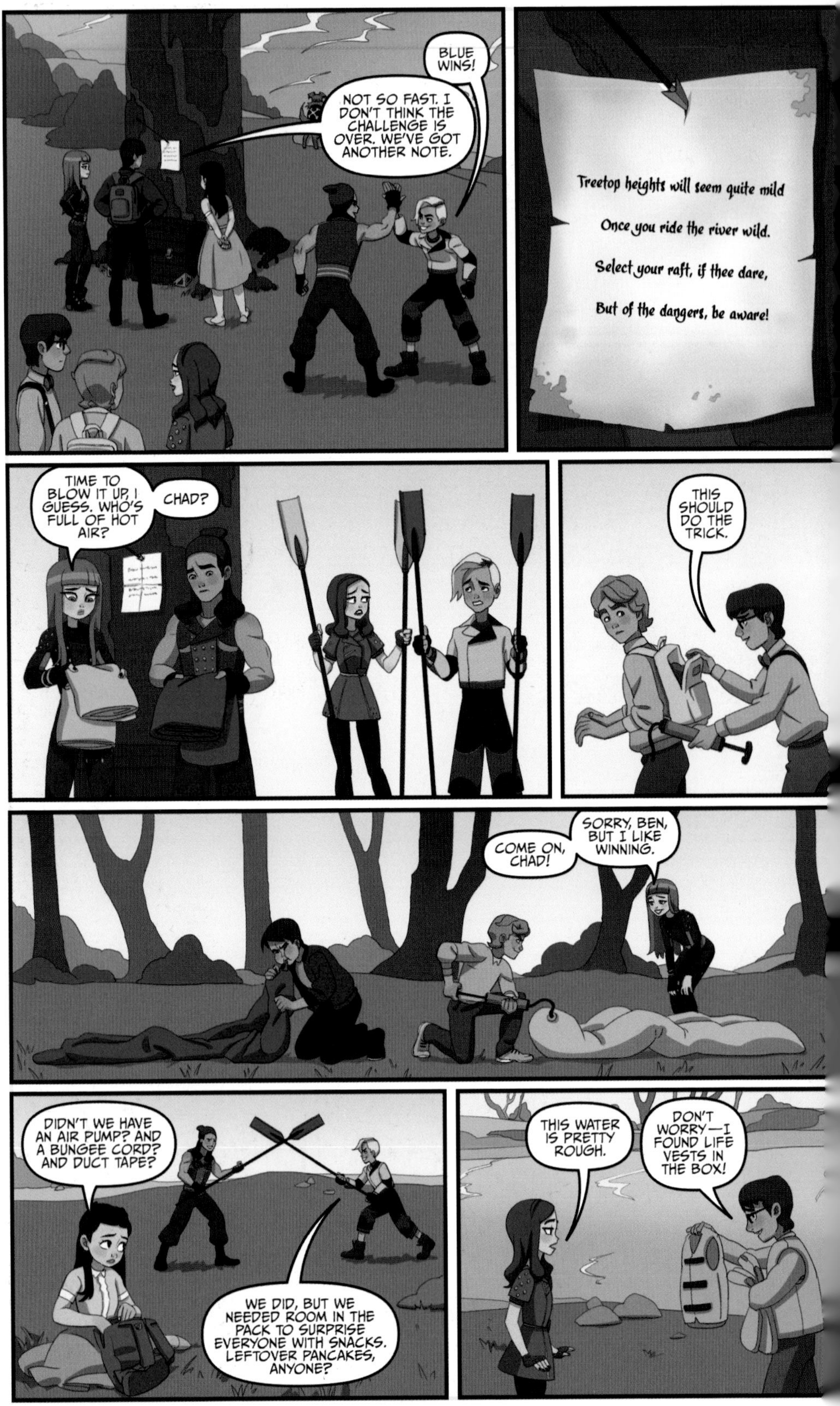
BLUE WINS!
NOT SO FAST. I DON'T THINK THE CHALLENGE IS OVER. WE'VE GOT ANOTHER NOTE.
Treetop heights will seem quite mild
Once you ride the river wild.
Select your raft, if thee dare,
But of the dangers, be aware!
TIME TO BLOW IT UP, I GUESS. WHO'S FULL OF HOT AIR?
CHAD?
THIS SHOULD DO THE TRICK.
COME ON, CHAD!
SORRY, BEN, BUT I LIKE WINNING.
DIDN'T WE HAVE AN AIR PUMP? AND A BUNGEE CORD? AND DUCT TAPE?
WE DID, BUT WE NEEDED ROOM IN THE PACK TO SURPRISE EVERYONE WITH SNACKS. LEFTOVER PANCAKES, ANYONE?
THIS WATER IS PRETTY ROUGH.
DON'T WORRY—I FOUND LIFE VESTS IN THE BOX!

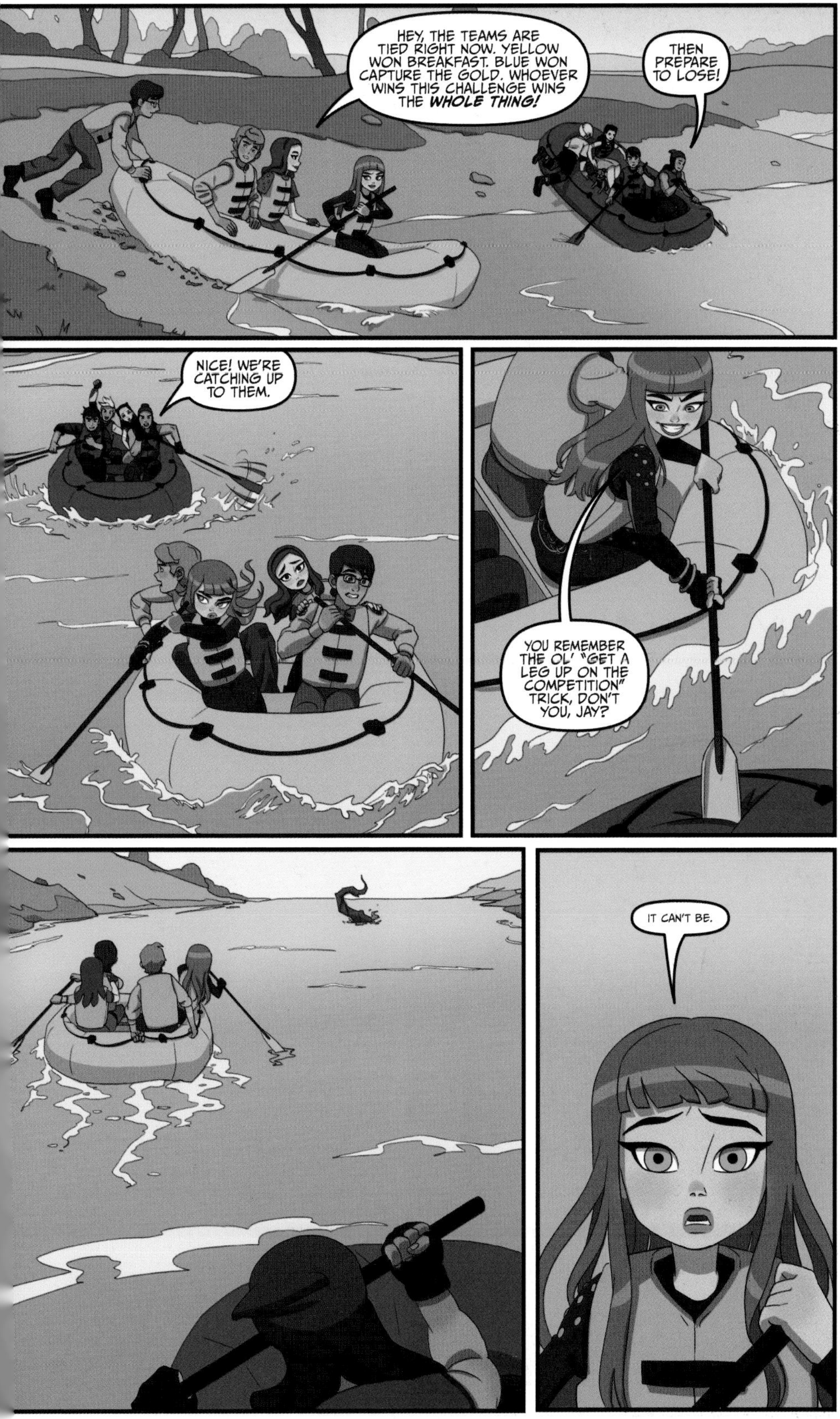
HEY, THE TEAMS ARE TIED RIGHT NOW. YELLOW WON BREAKFAST. BLUE WON CAPTURE THE GOLD. WHOEVER WINS THIS CHALLENGE WINS THE ***WHOLE THING!***
THEN PREPARE TO LOSE!
NICE! WE'RE CATCHING UP TO THEM.
YOU REMEMBER THE OL' "GET A LEG UP ON THE COMPETITION" TRICK, DON'T YOU, JAY?
IT CAN'T BE.

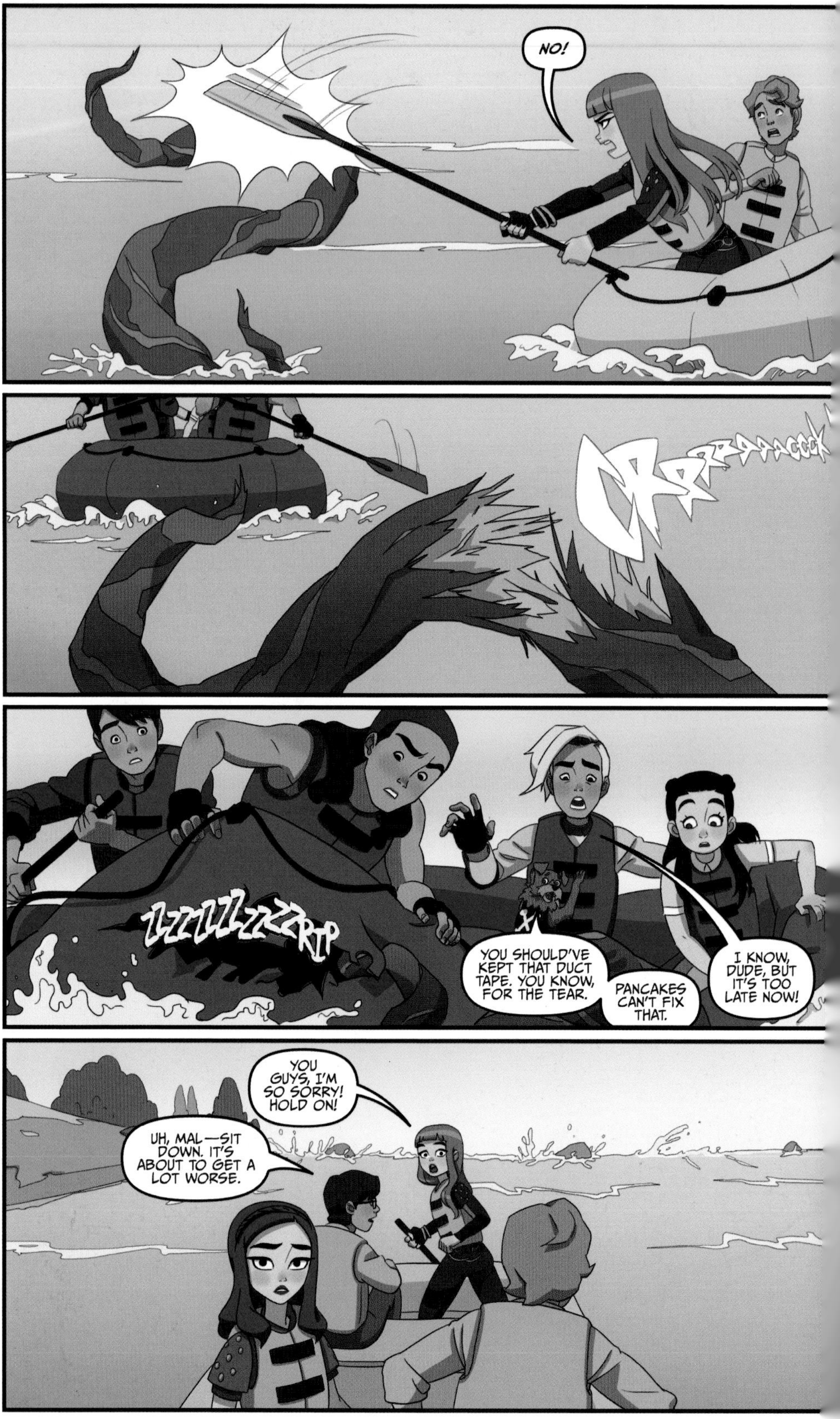
NO!
CRRRRRRACCCK
ZZZZZZZZZZRIP
YOU SHOULD'VE KEPT THAT DUCT TAPE. YOU KNOW, FOR THE TEAR.
PANCAKES CAN'T FIX THAT.
I KNOW, DUDE, BUT IT'S TOO LATE NOW!
YOU GUYS, I'M SO SORRY! HOLD ON!
UH, MAL—SIT DOWN. IT'S ABOUT TO GET A LOT WORSE.

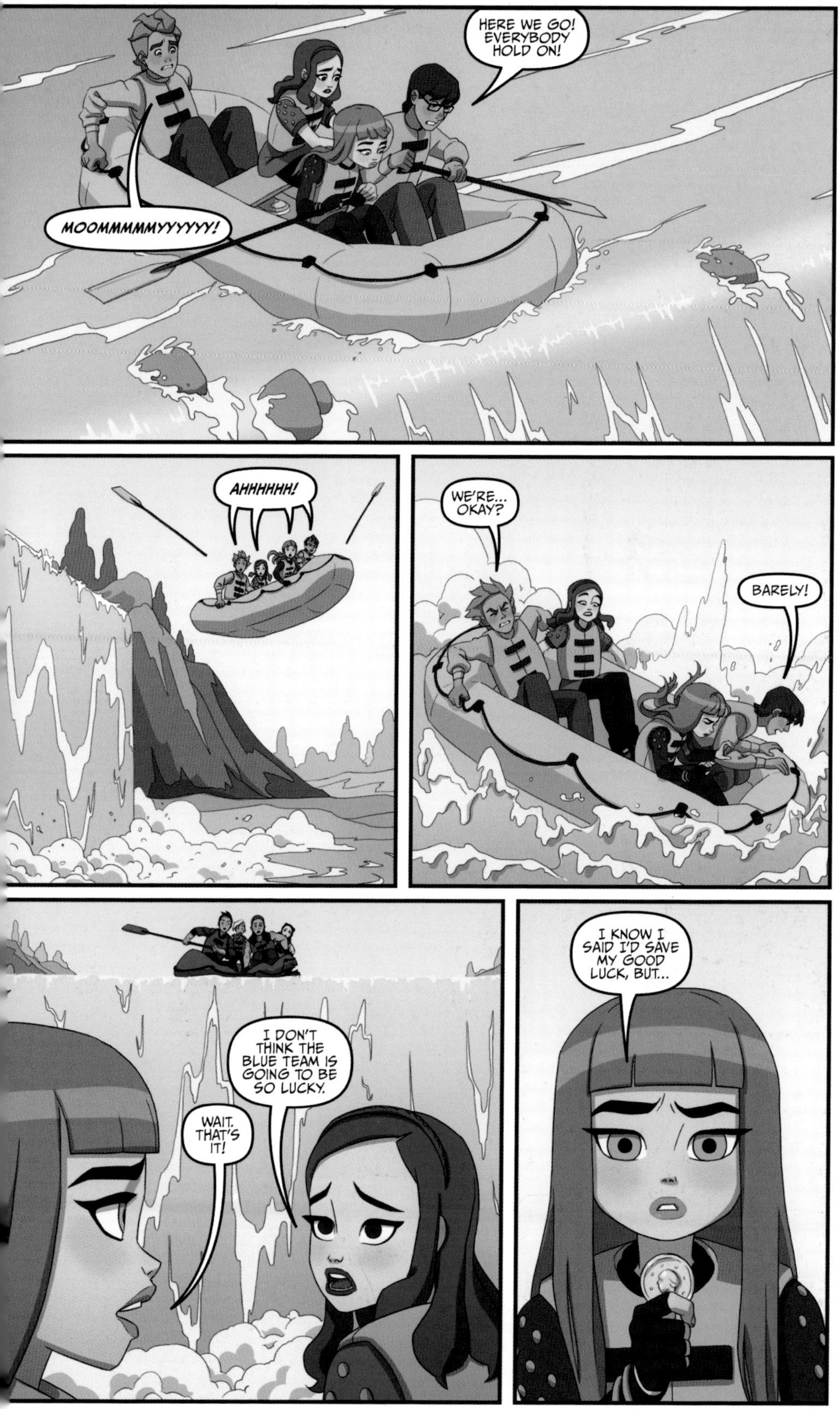
HERE WE GO! EVERYBODY HOLD ON!
MOOMMMMMYYYYYY!
AHHHHHH!
WE'RE... OKAY?
BARELY!
I DON'T THINK THE BLUE TEAM IS GOING TO BE SO LUCKY.
WAIT. THAT'S IT!
I KNOW I SAID I'D SAVE MY GOOD LUCK, BUT...

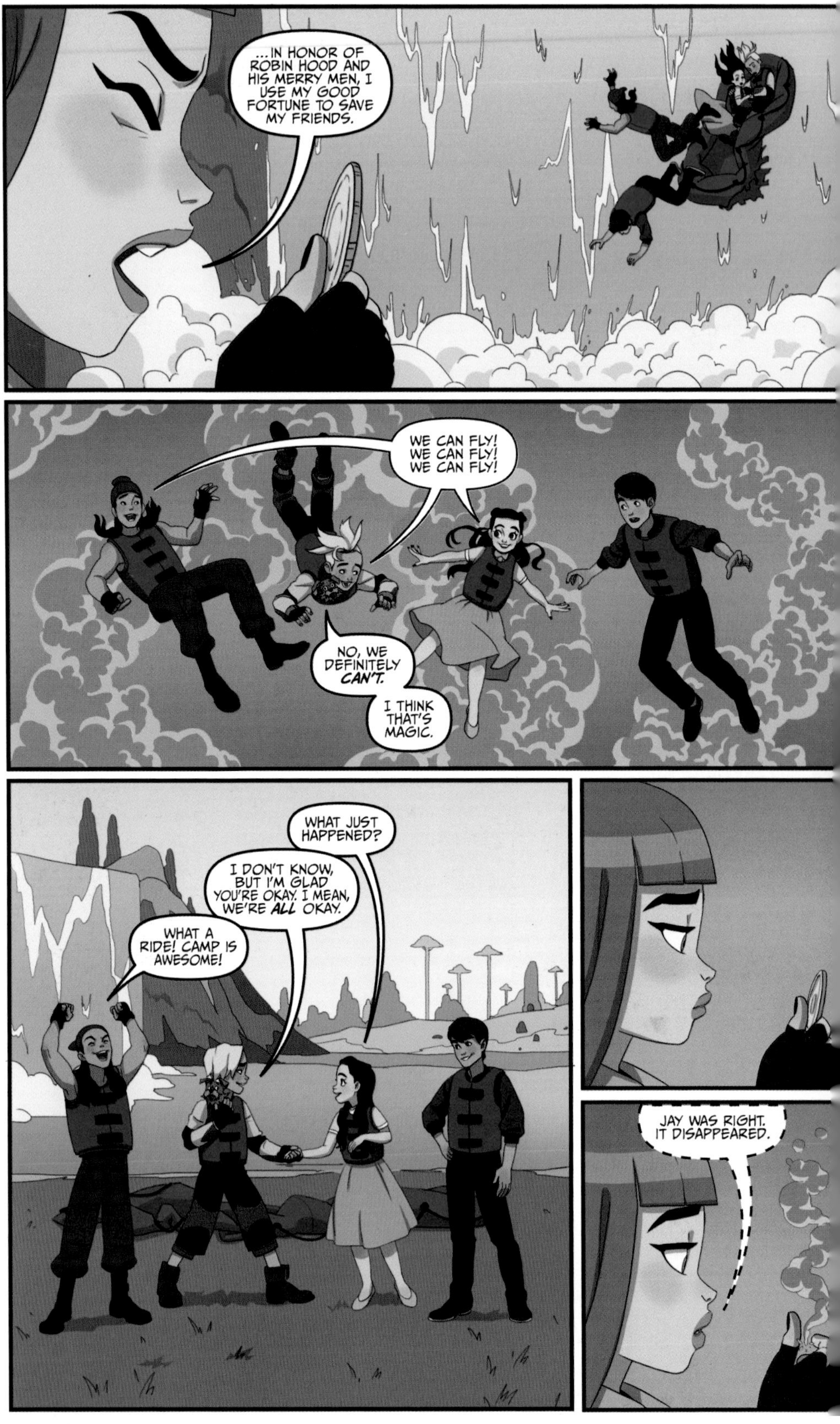
...IN HONOR OF ROBIN HOOD AND HIS MERRY MEN, I USE MY GOOD FORTUNE TO SAVE MY FRIENDS.
WE CAN FLY! WE CAN FLY! WE CAN FLY!
NO, WE DEFINITELY CAN'T.
I THINK THAT'S MAGIC.
WHAT JUST HAPPENED?
I DON'T KNOW, BUT I'M GLAD YOU'RE OKAY. I MEAN, WE'RE ALL OKAY.
WHAT A RIDE! CAMP IS AWESOME!
JAY WAS RIGHT. IT DISAPPEARED.

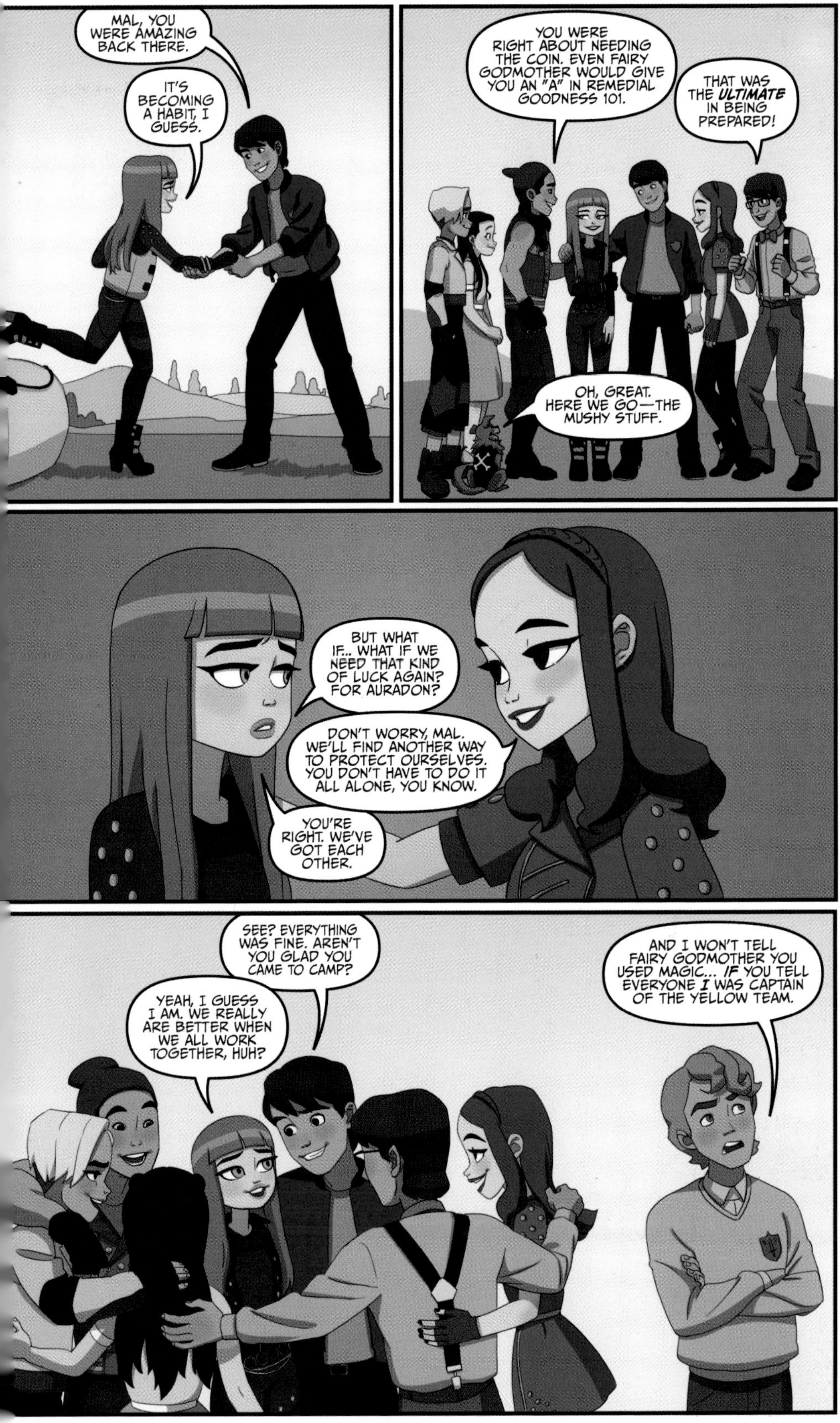
MAL, YOU WERE AMAZING BACK THERE.
IT'S BECOMING A HABIT, I GUESS.
YOU WERE RIGHT ABOUT NEEDING THE COIN. EVEN FAIRY GODMOTHER WOULD GIVE YOU AN "A" IN REMEDIAL GOODNESS 101.
THAT WAS THE *ULTIMATE* IN BEING PREPARED!
OH, GREAT. HERE WE GO—THE MUSHY STUFF.
BUT WHAT IF... WHAT IF WE NEED THAT KIND OF LUCK AGAIN? FOR AURADON?
DON'T WORRY, MAL. WE'LL FIND ANOTHER WAY TO PROTECT OURSELVES. YOU DON'T HAVE TO DO IT ALL ALONE, YOU KNOW.
YOU'RE RIGHT. WE'VE GOT EACH OTHER.
SEE? EVERYTHING WAS FINE. AREN'T YOU GLAD YOU CAME TO CAMP?
YEAH, I GUESS I AM. WE REALLY ARE BETTER WHEN WE ALL WORK TOGETHER, HUH?
AND I WON'T TELL FAIRY GODMOTHER YOU USED MAGIC... *IF* YOU TELL EVERYONE *I* WAS CAPTAIN OF THE YELLOW TEAM.

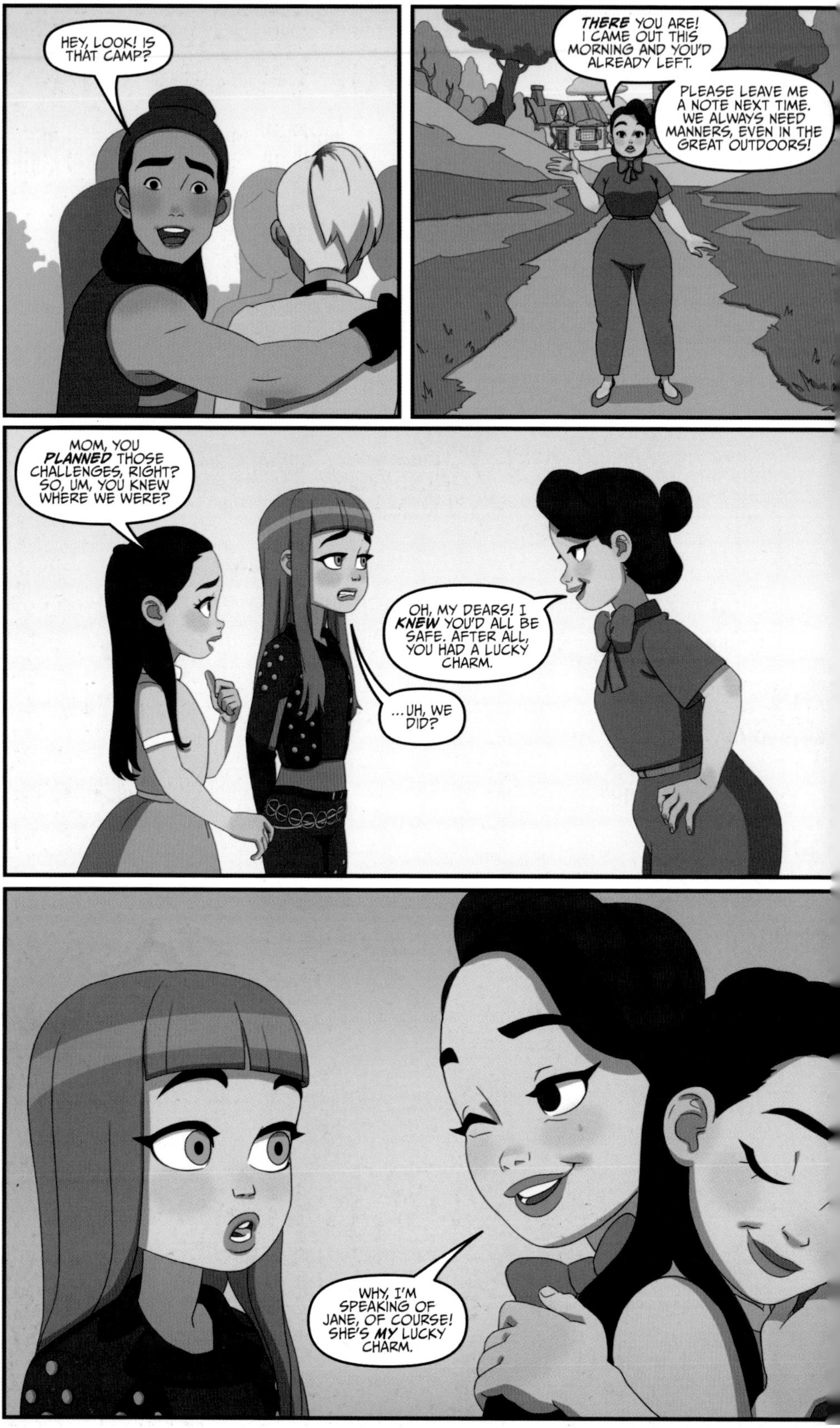
HEY, LOOK! IS THAT CAMP?
THERE YOU ARE! I CAME OUT THIS MORNING AND YOU'D ALREADY LEFT.
PLEASE LEAVE ME A NOTE NEXT TIME. WE ALWAYS NEED MANNERS, EVEN IN THE GREAT OUTDOORS!
MOM, YOU PLANNED THOSE CHALLENGES, RIGHT? SO, UM, YOU KNEW WHERE WE WERE?
OH, MY DEARS! I KNEW YOU'D ALL BE SAFE. AFTER ALL, YOU HAD A LUCKY CHARM.
...UH, WE DID?
WHY, I'M SPEAKING OF JANE, OF COURSE! SHE'S MY LUCKY CHARM.

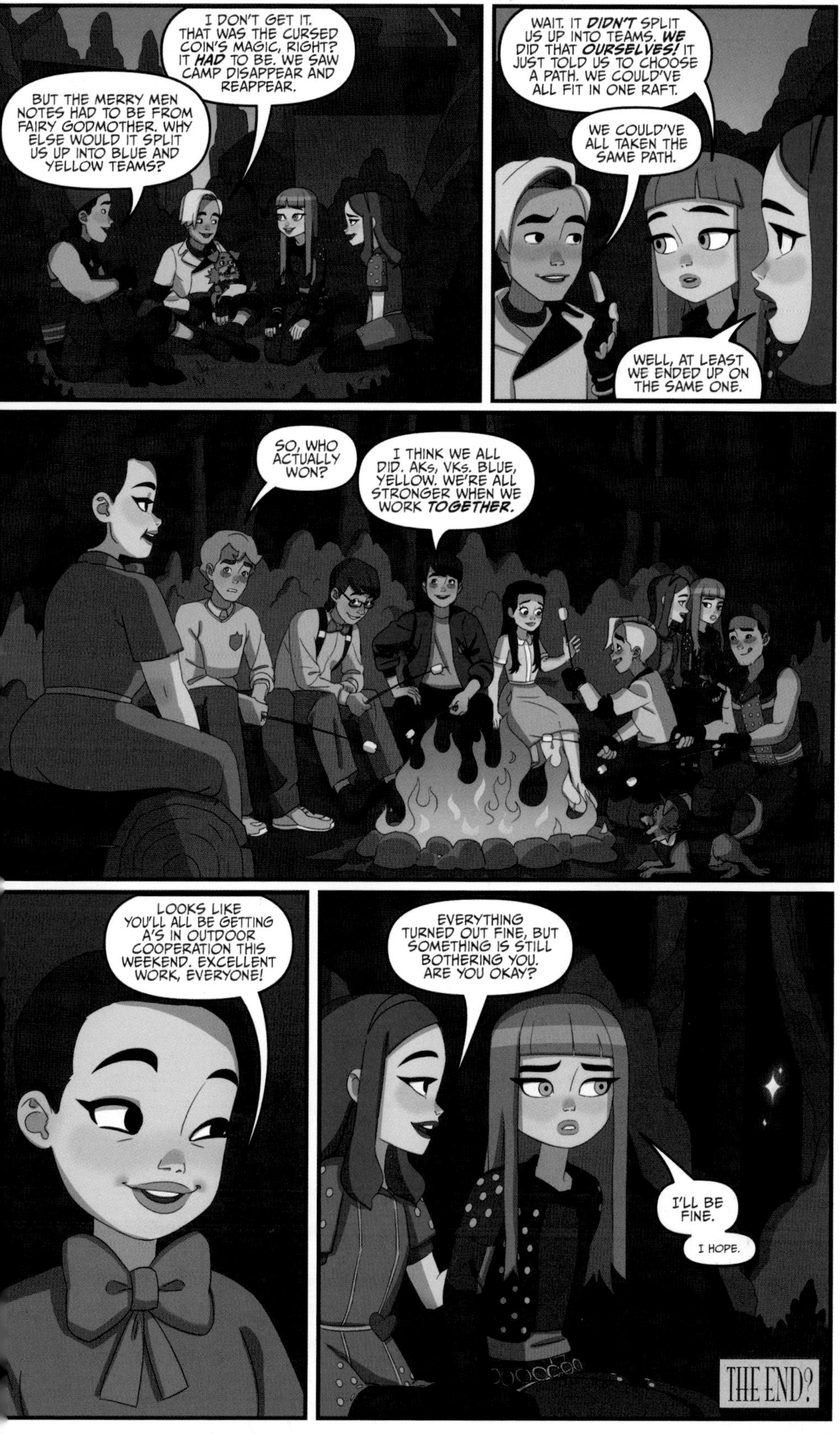

I DON'T GET IT. THAT WAS THE CURSED COIN'S MAGIC, RIGHT? IT HAD TO BE. WE SAW CAMP DISAPPEAR AND REAPPEAR.
BUT THE MERRY MEN NOTES HAD TO BE FROM FAIRY GODMOTHER. WHY ELSE WOULD IT SPLIT US UP INTO BLUE AND YELLOW TEAMS?
WAIT. IT DIDN'T SPLIT US UP INTO TEAMS. WE DID THAT OURSELVES! IT JUST TOLD US TO CHOOSE A PATH. WE COULD'VE ALL FIT IN ONE RAFT.
WE COULD'VE ALL TAKEN THE SAME PATH.
WELL, AT LEAST WE ENDED UP ON THE SAME ONE.
SO, WHO ACTUALLY WON?
I THINK WE ALL DID. AKs, VKs. BLUE, YELLOW. WE'RE ALL STRONGER WHEN WE WORK TOGETHER.
LOOKS LIKE YOU'LL ALL BE GETTING A'S IN OUTDOOR COOPERATION THIS WEEKEND. EXCELLENT WORK, EVERYONE!
EVERYTHING TURNED OUT FINE, BUT SOMETHING IS STILL BOTHERING YOU. ARE YOU OKAY?
I'LL BE FINE.
I HOPE.
THE END?

HOW THIS GRAPHIC NOVEL WAS MADE!

WE FOUND SO MANY WAYS TO BE WICKED WHILE MAKING *DESCENDANTS: TWISTED FIELD TRIP*. FROM CHARACTER DESIGNS TO LETTERING, THE AMAZING TEAM WORKED TOGETHER TO BRING EVERYONE'S FAVORITE VILLAIN KIDS AND AURADON KIDS TO LIFE—AS COMIC BOOK CHARACTERS!

CHARACTER DESIGNS

ANNA CATTISH DESIGNED ALL THE CHARACTERS FOR *DESCENDANTS: TWISTED FIELD TRIP*. SHE WORKED HARD TO CREATE JUST THE RIGHT LOOK TO CAPTURE THE AURADAN SPIRIT—AND TO MAKE SURE THE VKs HAD ALL THE ATTITUDE THEY NEED TO KEEP THEM CHILLIN' LIKE VILLAINS!

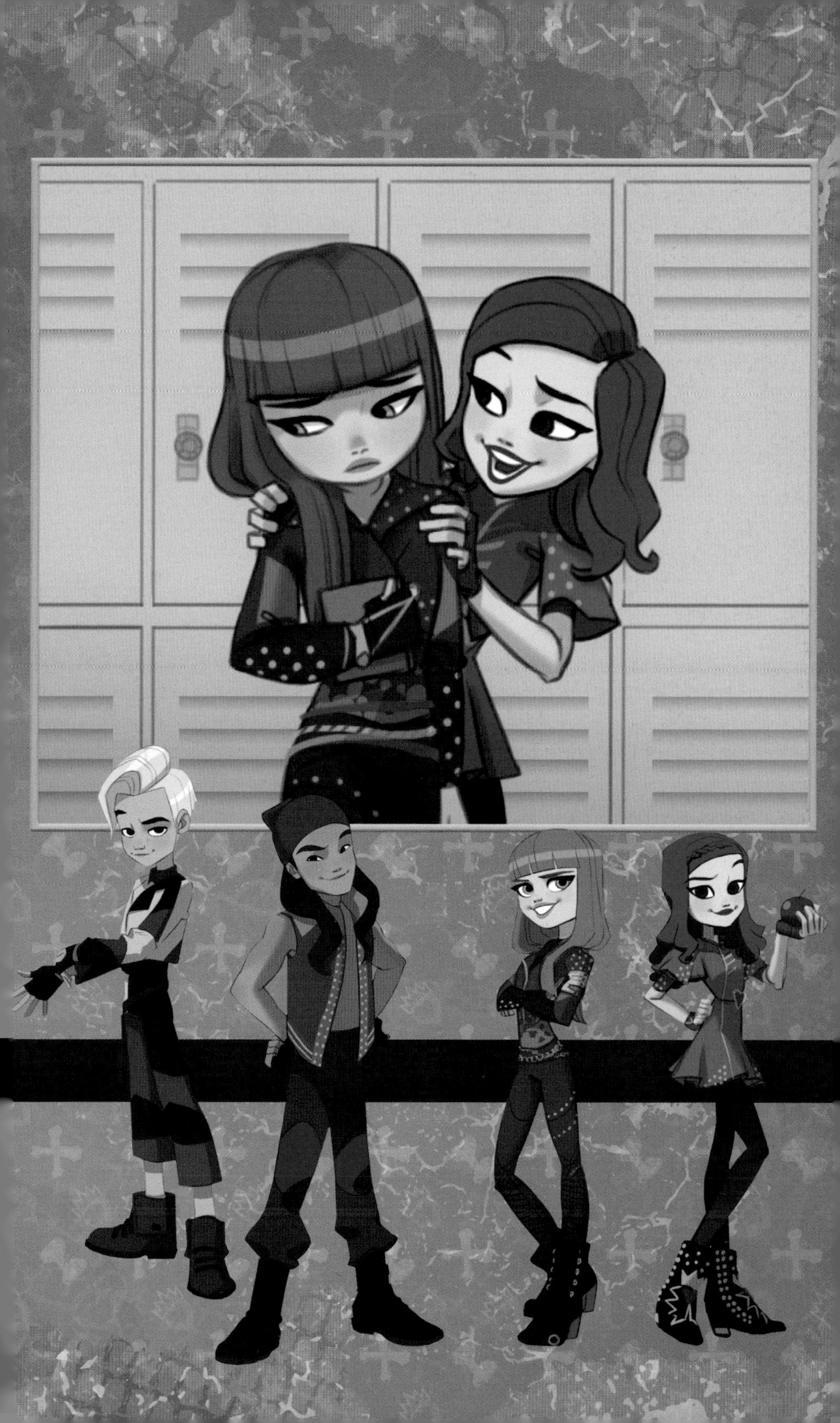

PAGE 25

Panel 1

Jay tags Ben and Carlos out of the yellow jail in the horse stall. In the distance, Chad sees him and throws up his arms (still holding the skillet) and shouts as Jane is about to make her move.

1. CHAD

Oh, no—jailbreak!

Panel 2

Inset. In a shadow in the stable, Jay passes Carlos the real yellow bag and winks, keeping the decoy yellow bag himself. Carlos grins.

Panel 3

Jay makes a big show of running with the decoy yellow bag in plain sight. Evie and Doug are running in toward him from the forest, yellow bows and arrows ready.

2. JAY

Yes, I got the yellow bag! I rule!

3. DOUG

Hey, not so fast!

Panel 4

Evie and Doug both hit Jay with yellow paint arrows-- they both look super proud of themselves. Jay holds his hands up in an 'Oh no, you got me' way while grinning that Jay grin.

DELILAH DAWSON AND CARIN DAVIS WORKED TOGETHER TO WRITE A SCRIPT FOR THE COMIC. THIS SCRIPT INCLUDES THE PANEL DESCRIPTIONS, WHICH ARE THE BOXES IN WHICH THE ACTION HAPPENS, AND THE DIALOGUE EACH OF THE CHARACTERS SAYS. IT'S A LITTLE LIKE A MOVIE SCRIPT!

4. SFX (Evie's arrow)

Splat

5. SFX (Doug's arrow)

Splurt

6. JAY

Oh no, you got me! I'm *sooo* upset...

Panel 5

Close up of the fake yellow bag falling apart on the ground at Jay's feet.

7. JAY (from off-panel)

...Just kidding. You got **played**!

Panel 6

Ben and Carlos stand at the tree with the map/sign on it, on the blue territory side. Carlos holds up the real yellow bag, his other hand on the map.

8. CARLOS

We won, **and** we got pancakes! Best day **ever**!

...her smiles, a finger up as she imparts her wis...
...nd watch her.

7. FAIRY GODMOTHER

...be **early** tonight, my dears. We have a big day...

...cabin at twilight. Jane is asleep in her bunk.
...ottom bunk, whispering, lit by the single lant...
...in the cabin than outside). Lots of purple sh...

...een thinking. Maybe we should look for Prince John's cursed c...

8. MAL

9. EVIE

Wait... from Jane's ghost story?

Panel 5

Mal's moment of confession and vulnerability. Close up of Mal, concerned.
Evie looks open and understanding, BFF forever.

If Jane's story is true and the coin has powers, then maybe it will be...

10.   MAL

...lpful if something bad happens. Like Uma returning. If she comes back, I...
...need to be ready to protect Auradon.

PENCILS

ANNA DREW ROUGH SKETCHES OF THE PANELS TO
GET A FEEL FOR HOW THE PAGES WOULD LOOK. SHE
WORKED WITH THE EDITORS AND WRITERS TO MAKE
ADJUSTMENTS TO MAKE SURE THE STORYTELLING
WAS CLEAR AND EVERYTHING MADE SENSE!

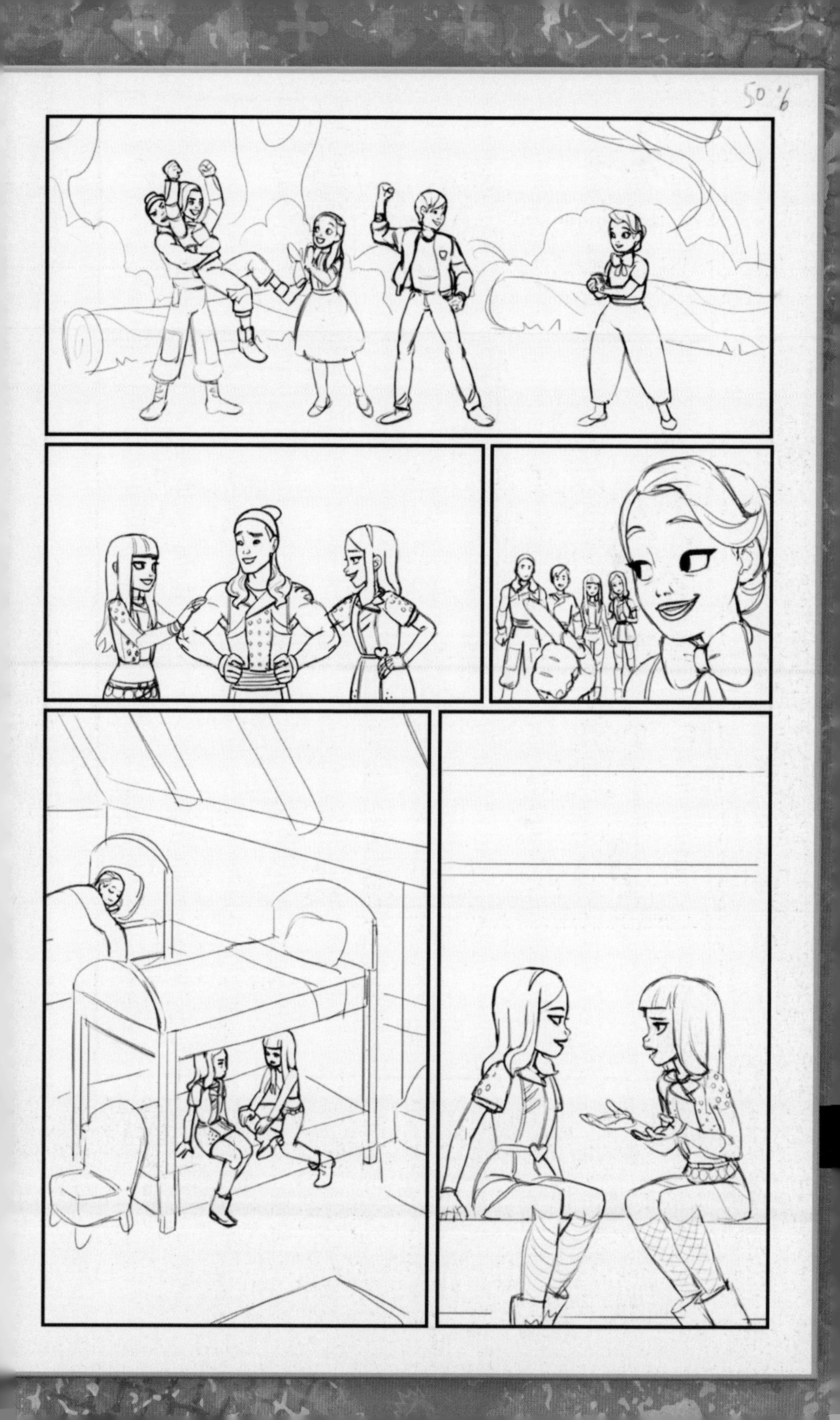

INKS

ONCE EVERYONE AGREED THAT THE PAGES LOOKED RIGHT FROM A STORYTELLING PERSPECTIVE, ANNA DREW OVER THE LINES WITH INK. AT THIS STAGE, ANNA REFINED ALL THE DETAILS OF THE CHARACTERS AND BACKGROUNDS AND MADE SURE EVERYTHING WAS PROPORTIONATE.

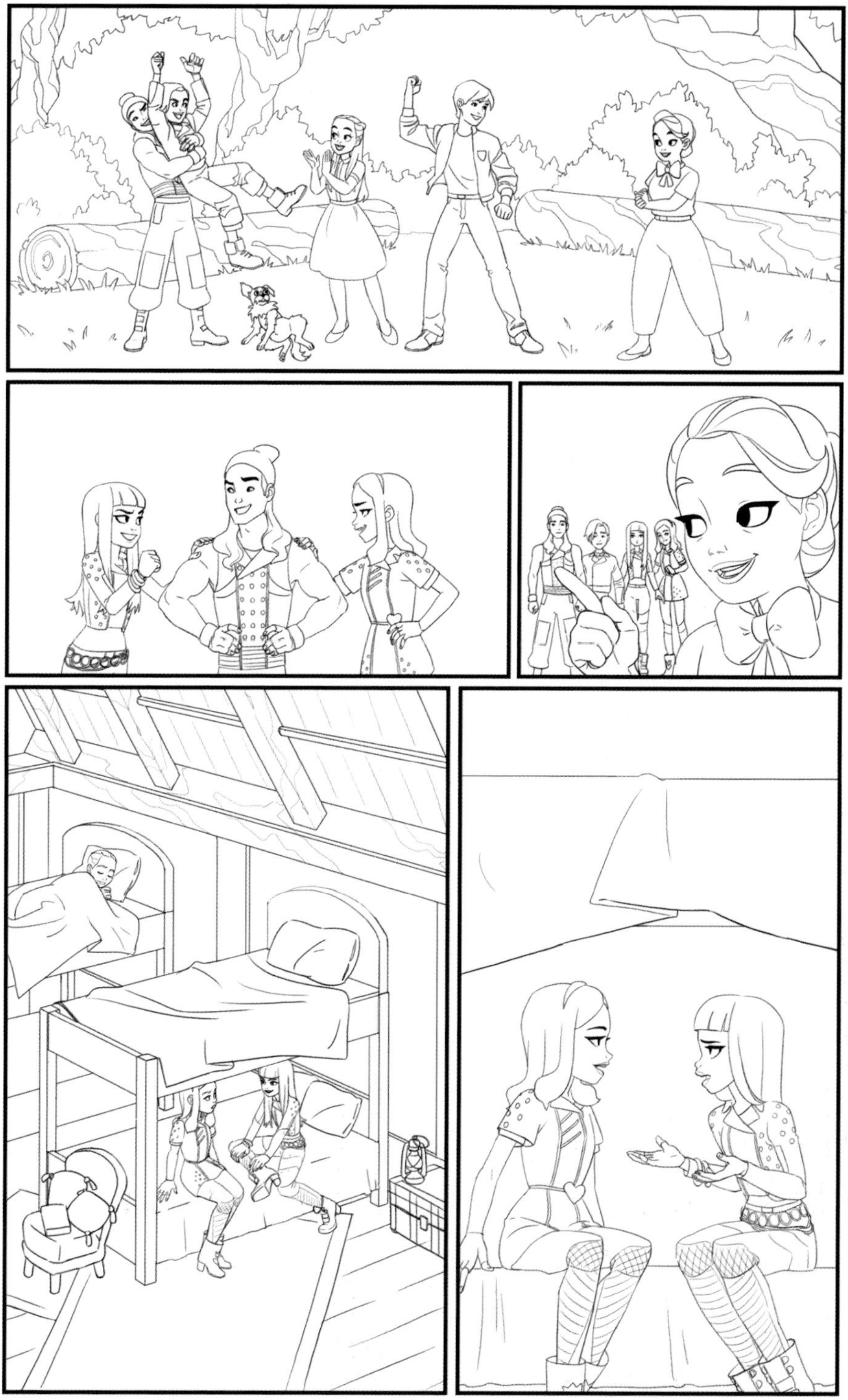

COLORS

ONCE THE INKS WERE FINISHED, ANNA MOVED ON TO THE FINAL ART STEP—COLORS! COLOR MAKES THE PAGE MORE VIBRANT AND FUN TO LOOK AT, BUT IT IS ALSO USED TO ADD DEPTH AND DETAIL TO PANELS (LIKE THE SHADOWS OF TREES OR PEOPLE) AND HELPS DEFINE THE FACIAL EXPRESSIONS OF THE CHARACTERS.

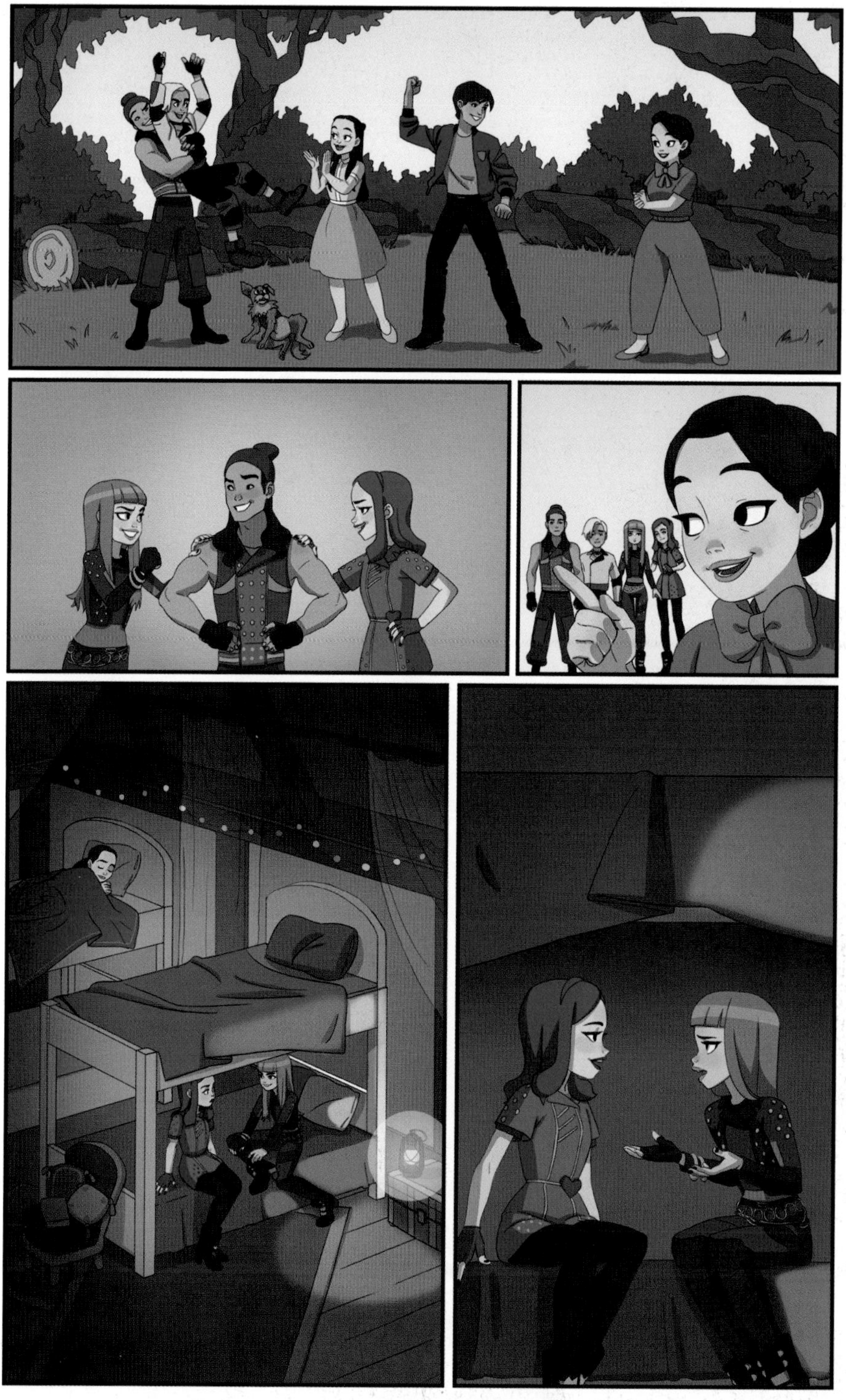

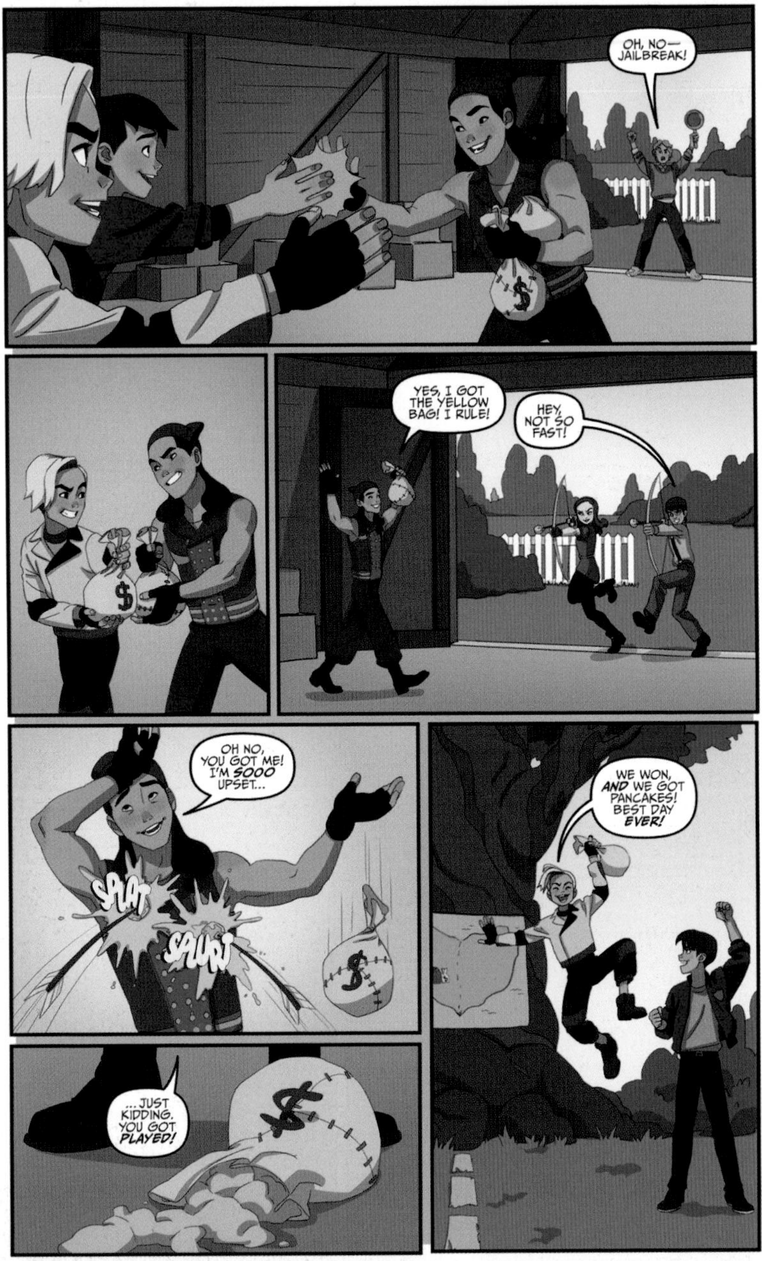
OH, NO—
JAILBREAK!
YES, I GOT THE YELLOW BAG! I RULE!
HEY, NOT SO FAST!
OH NO, YOU GOT ME! I'M *SOOO* UPSET...
SPLAT
SPLURT
...JUST KIDDING. YOU GOT *PLAYED!*
WE WON, *AND* WE GOT PANCAKES! BEST DAY *EVER!*

LETTERS

FROM HERE, CHRISTA MIESNER TOOK THE WORDS FROM DELILAH AND CARIN'S SCRIPT AND SHAPED THEM INTO BALLOONS AND CAPTIONS, GIVING THE CHARACTERS THE WORDS THAT THEY'D SAY! A PAGE ISN'T COMPLETE UNTIL IT'S BEEN IN A LETTERER'S HANDS!

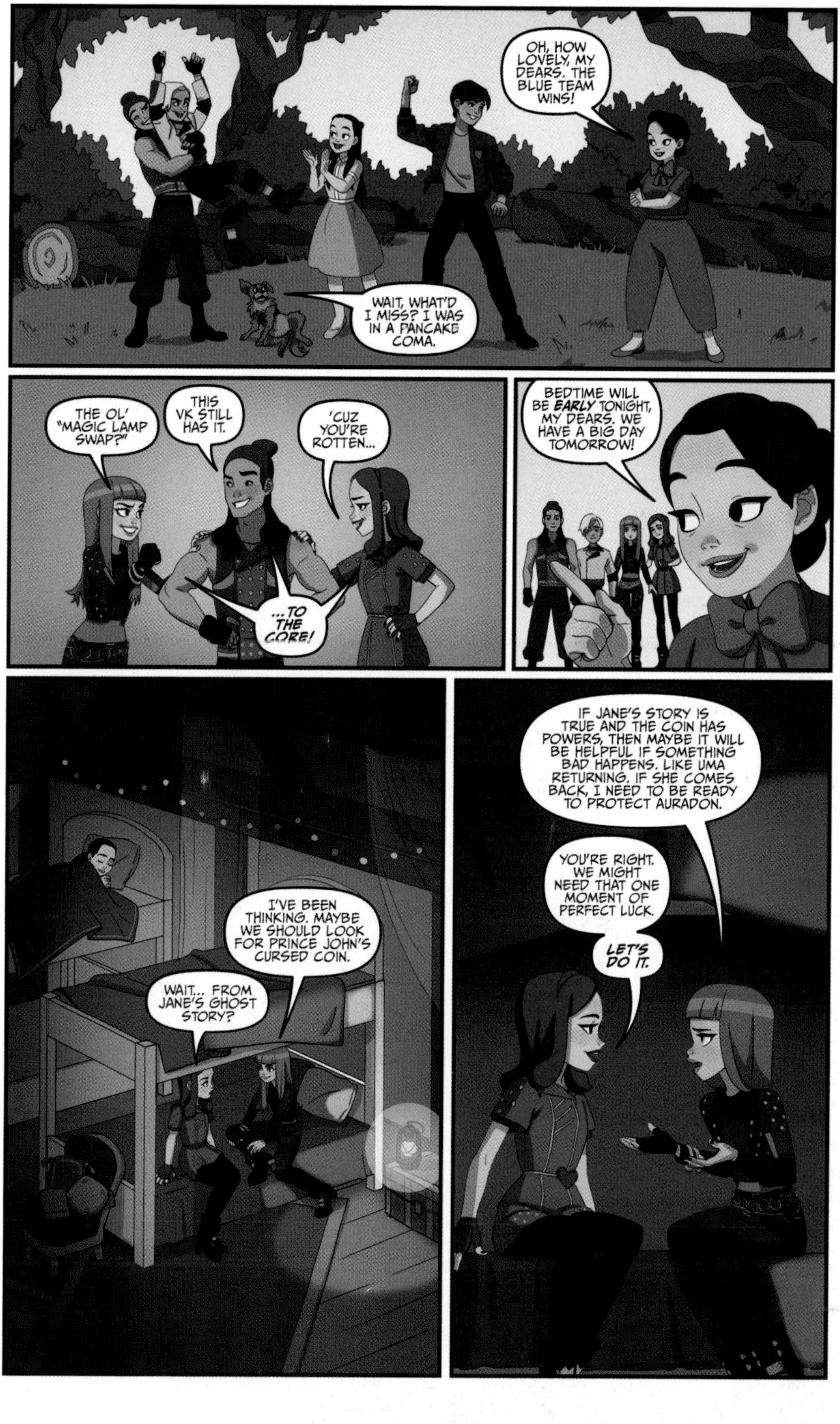

OH, HOW LOVELY, MY DEARS. THE BLUE TEAM WINS!
WAIT, WHAT'D I MISS? I WAS IN A PANCAKE COMA.
THE OL' "MAGIC LAMP SWAP?"
THIS VK STILL HAS IT.
'CUZ YOU'RE ROTTEN...
...TO THE CORE!
BEDTIME WILL BE EARLY TONIGHT, MY DEARS. WE HAVE A BIG DAY TOMORROW!
I'VE BEEN THINKING. MAYBE WE SHOULD LOOK FOR PRINCE JOHN'S CURSED COIN.
WAIT... FROM JANE'S GHOST STORY?
IF JANE'S STORY IS TRUE AND THE COIN HAS POWERS, THEN MAYBE IT WILL BE HELPFUL IF SOMETHING BAD HAPPENS. LIKE UMA RETURNING. IF SHE COMES BACK, I NEED TO BE READY TO PROTECT AURADON.
YOU'RE RIGHT. WE MIGHT NEED THAT ONE MOMENT OF PERFECT LUCK.
LET'S DO IT.

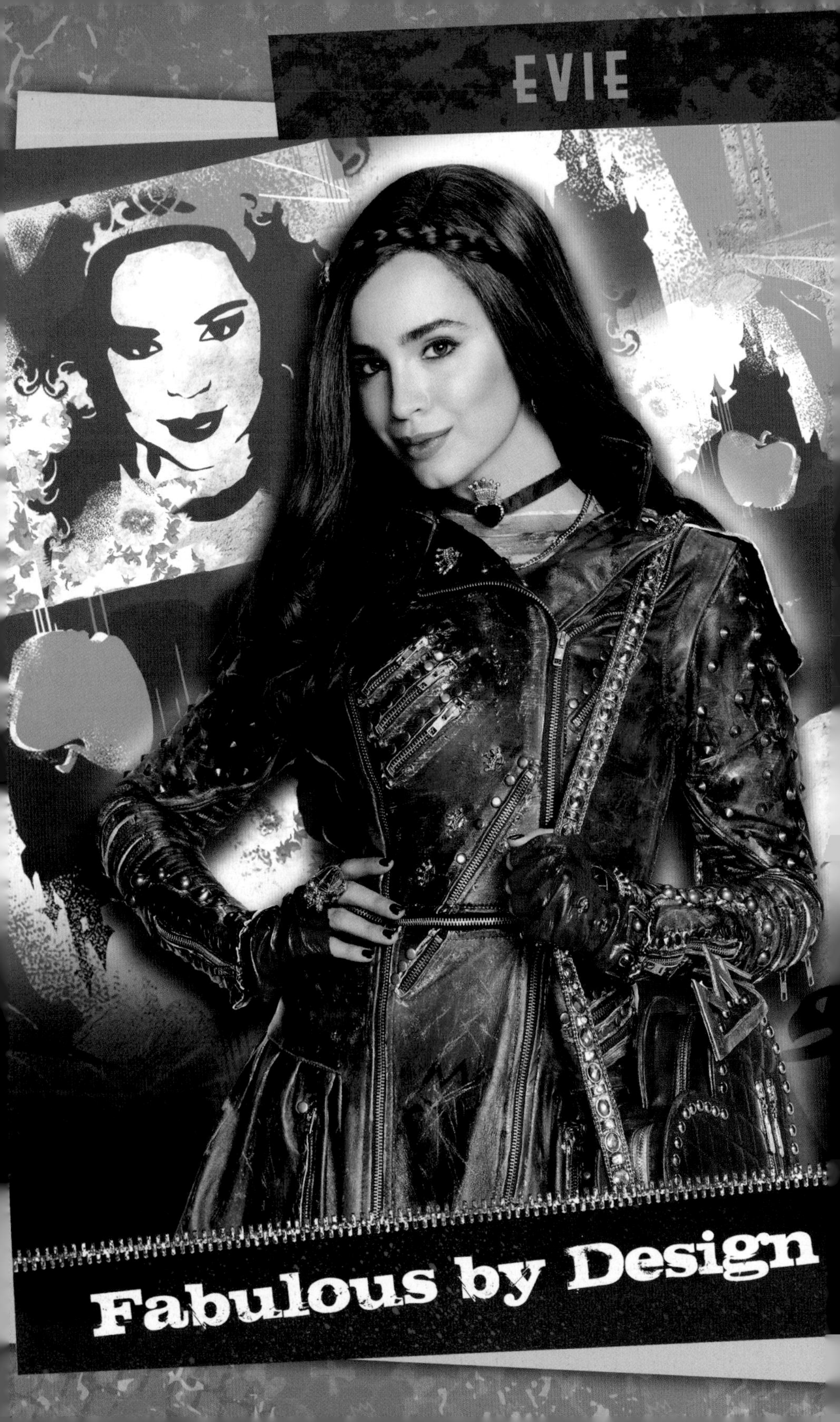
EVIE
Fabulous by Design

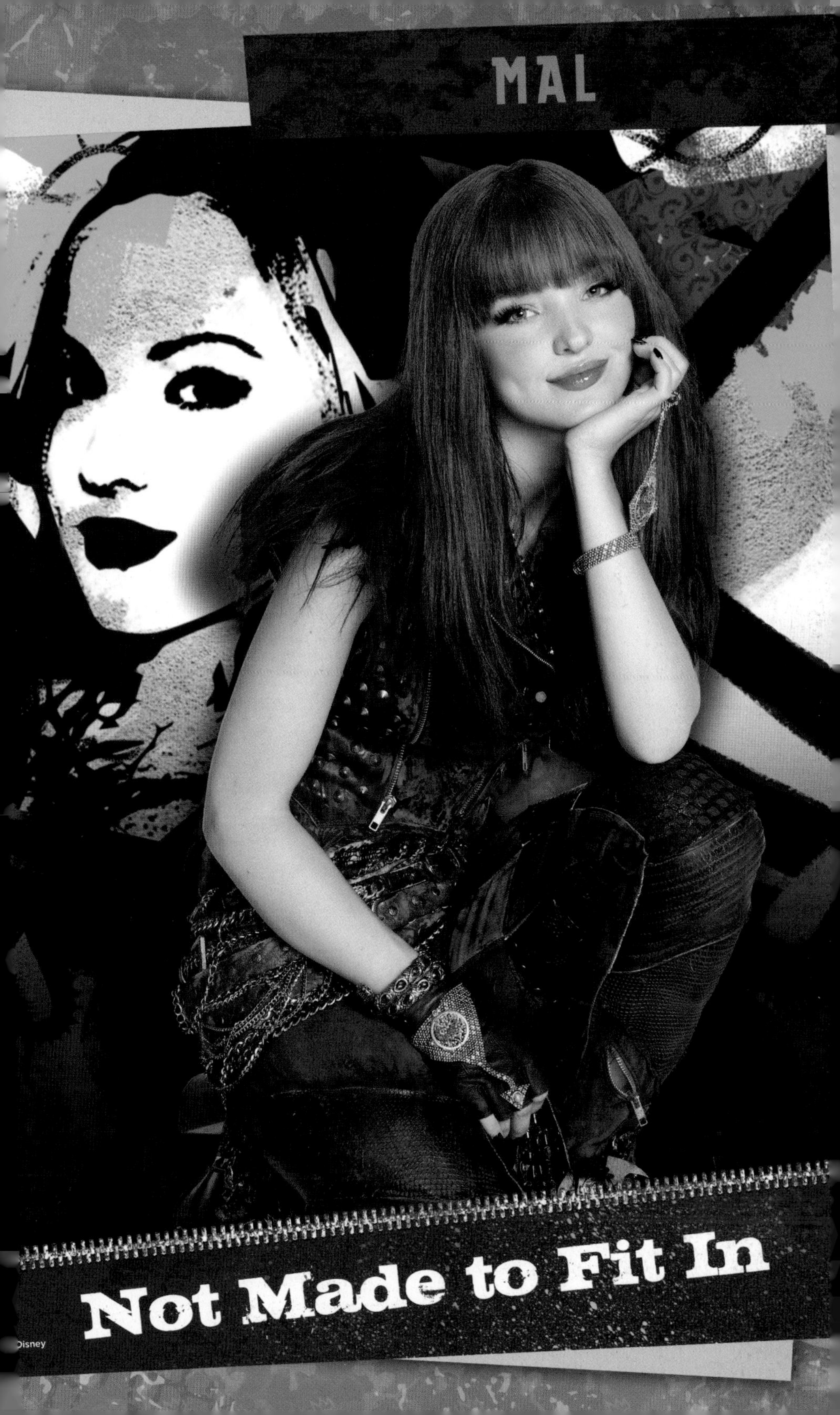
MAL
Not Made to Fit In
Disney

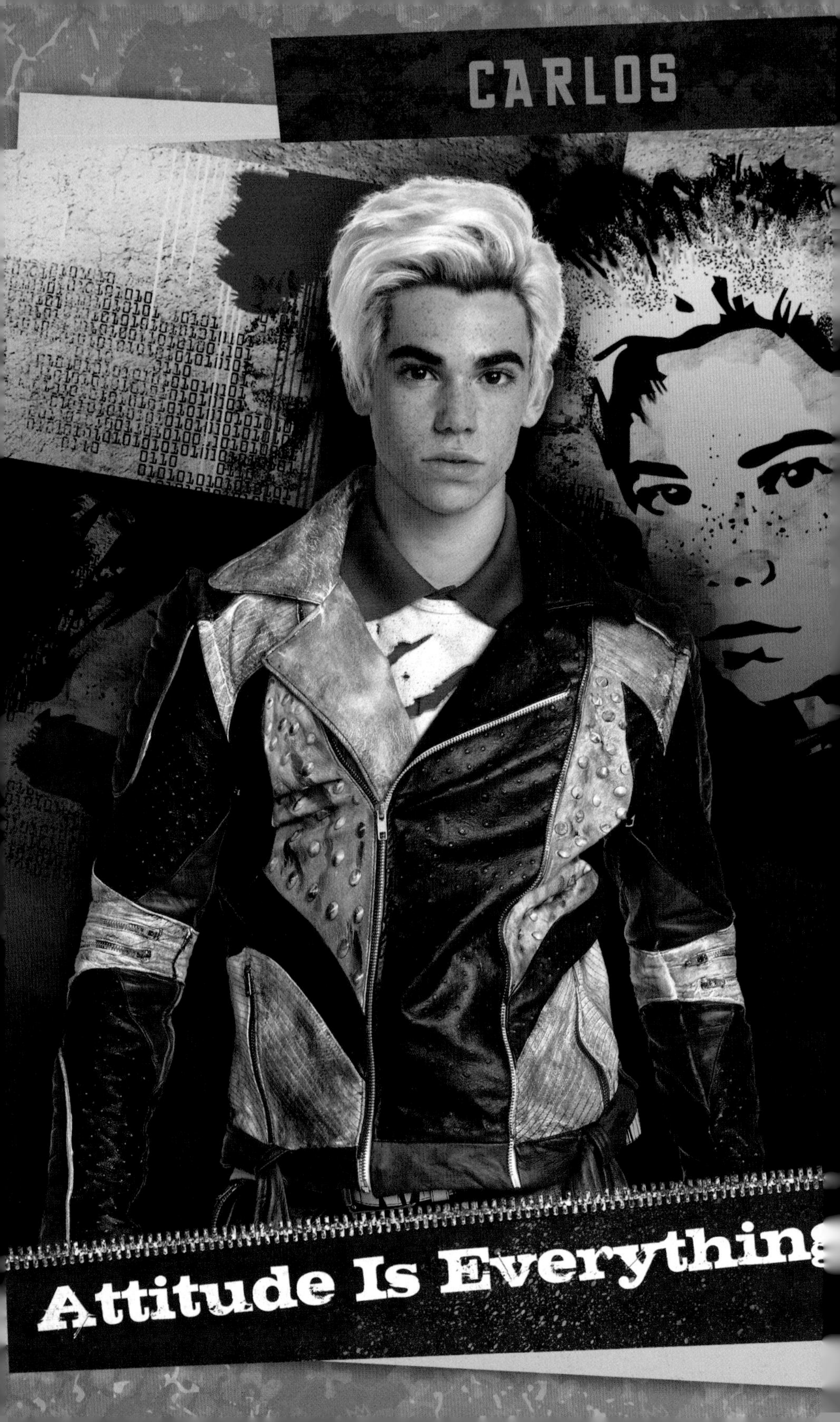
CARLOS
Attitude Is Everything

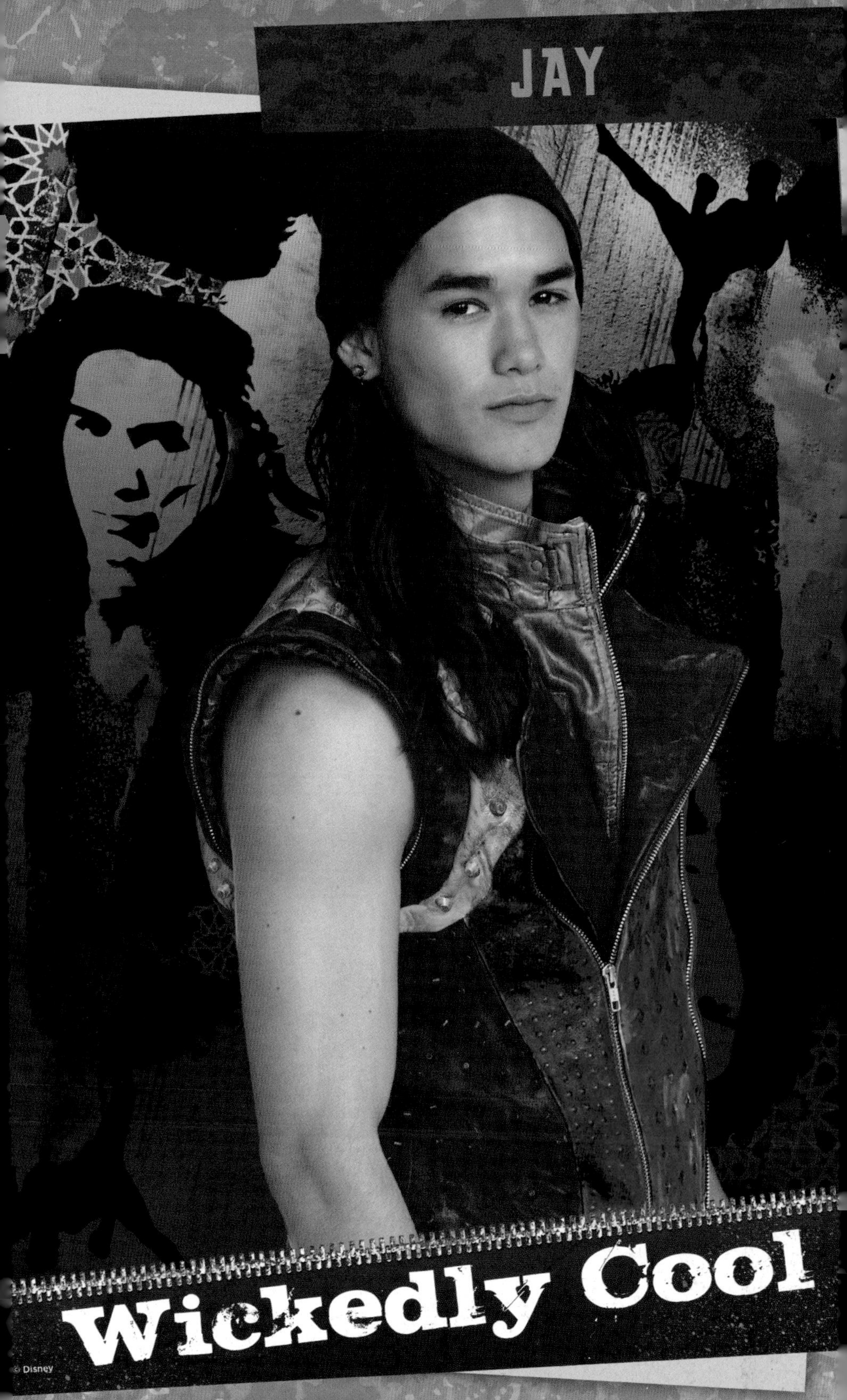
JAY
Wickedly Cool
© Disney

VKs

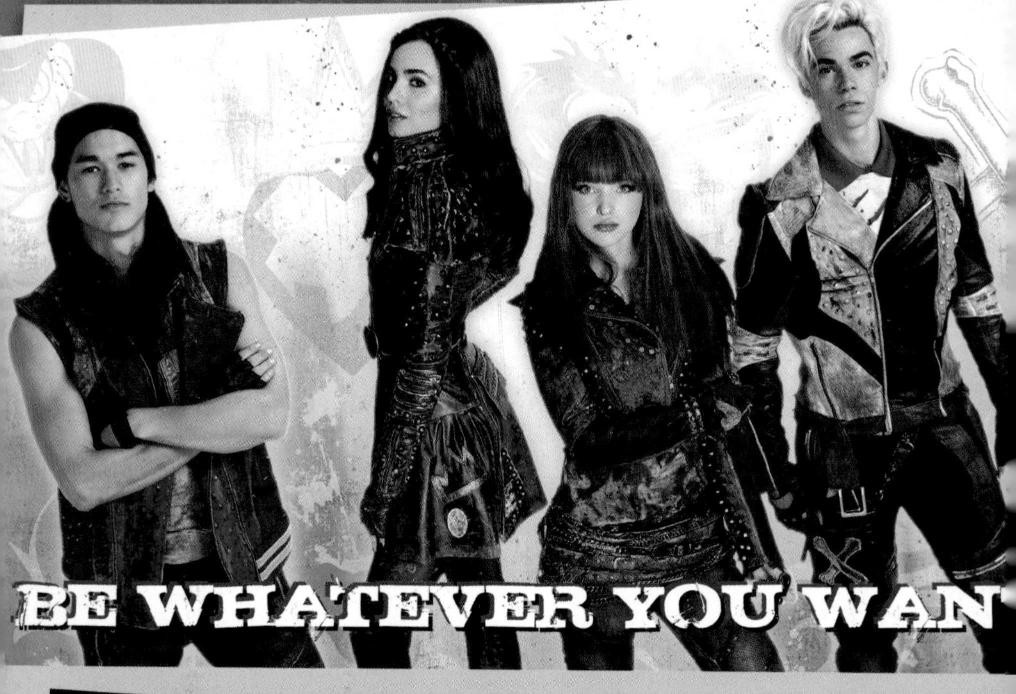
BE WHATEVER YOU WAN

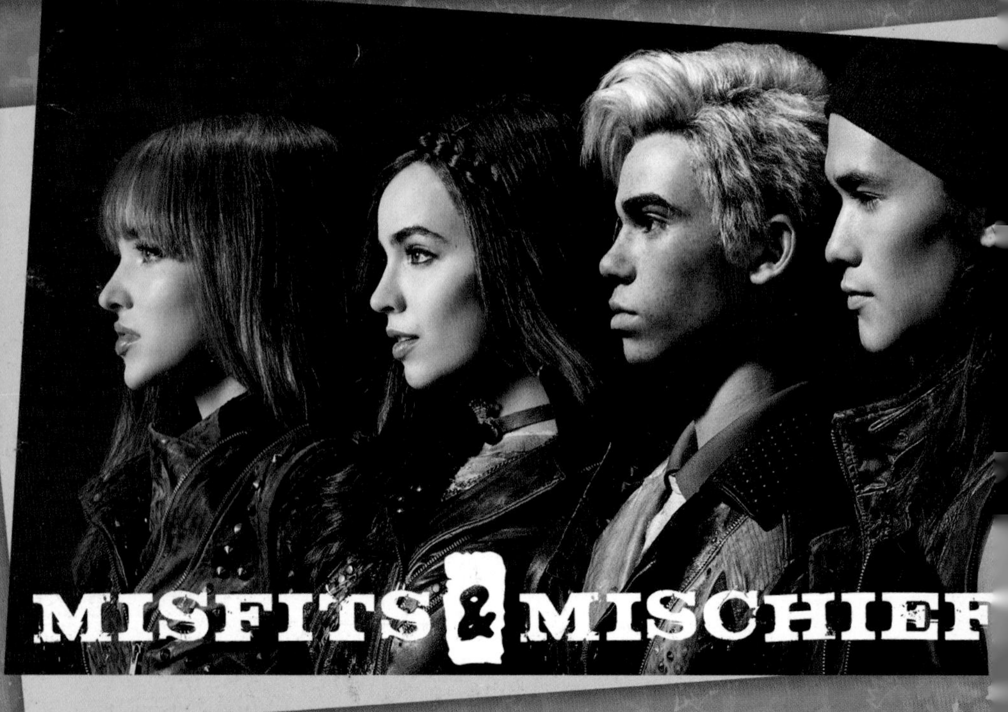
MISFITS & MISCHIEF